J. H. Needell

**Passing the Love of Women**

A Novel

J. H. Needell

**Passing the Love of Women**
*A Novel*

ISBN/EAN: 9783337294533

Printed in Europe, USA, Canada, Australia, Japan

Cover: Foto ©Andreas Hilbeck / pixelio.de

More available books at **www.hansebooks.com**

# PASSING THE LOVE OF WOMEN.

## A Novel.

BY

## MRS. J. H. NEEDELL,

AUTHOR OF

'STEPHEN ELLICOTT'S DAUGHTER,' 'THE STORY OF PHILIP METHUEN,' &TC.

IN THREE VOLUMES.

VOL. II.

LONDON:

FREDERICK WARNE AND CO.

AND NEW YORK.

1892.

# CONTENTS OF VOL. II.

# PASSING THE LOVE OF WOMEN.

## CHAPTER XIV.

### COUSINS.

THE travellers did not reach Rookhurst till late in the evening, long after the hour when Edward Yorke was accustomed to go to bed; but he had announced his resolution of sitting up in order to see his cousin, 'even if he had to wait up all night for it,' his pertinacity causing his mother some anxiety.

Sir Owen had arrived apparently in the best of spirits and of tempers, and had sat long over the exquisite little repast which his *chef* had solicitously prepared. He complimented his daughter-in-law in terms of such flagrant flattery that she coloured with indignation, and blushed deeper still when she saw that Gilbert blushed too.

Never, indeed, had Gilbert felt so uncomfortable. He had been introduced to his aunt with so much ceremony and importance that he felt it could only appear to her like provocation and insult, and he had hardly been permitted to speak to his cousin Philippa.

Sir Owen had greeted the girl with that sort of exaggerated deference with which he was apt to point his real contempt, and her mother had come to her relief by sending her away to keep her brother company.

But she carried away with her a new sensation. Gilbert had rushed to open the door for her, and, taking her hand as she passed out, he had put it to his lips with a few words of friendly kindness, and with his brown eyes alight with the same emotion.

It was in a tremor of excited feeling that poor Philippa sank down by her brother's couch and prepared to answer his eager questions about the stranger. The boy, as he listened to her, twisted and writhed as he was accustomed to do in the throes of physical pain; but on this occasion his suffering was mental. Was he to blame that his moral nature was as narrow and meagre as his bodily frame and intelligence? It would have needed sustained and almost divine patience to have developed in his mind—preoccupied from the cradle with his own pitiful individuality, and further spoiled by injudicious indulgence — the high and unselfish virtues.

When, a short time after, Gilbert entered his room with Mrs. Yorke, and walked straight up to his couch with his hand stretched out and pity in his eyes, Edward locked his hands together, and refused the friendly greeting.

His eyes had seized with a sort of desperate eagerness all the points of his cousin's person, and the result had inflamed his animosity. It was seldom that his countenance was so alert, but the expression of it was like that of a beaten hound which snarls where it dare not bite.

'I only shake hands with my friends,' he muttered. 'You and I are not likely to be that.'

'Then it will be your fault. I have the best will in the world to be friends with you.'

'It will take more than that,' sneered the boy. 'Mother, I will go to bed.'

Gilbert drew back with head erect. His temper was sweet, but he had not the forbearance of a saint, and he thought his cousin simply odious ; added to which, disease and infirmity always excited in his mind an instinctive recoil that it needed a moral effort to overcome.

'I, too, am very tired,' he said, turning to his aunt, 'and should like to go to my room ;' and then seeing Philippa, who was sitting on a low chair in the shadow of the brother's couch, he added : ' I hope you do not sit up at night.'

Edward stirred restlessly. The sympathetic voice roused his resentment.

' And if she does,' he said roughly, ' is that any business of yours ? You are not master of Rookhurst yet.'

Gilbert smiled, the poor fellow's spite seemed so gratuitous and so pitiful.

' I wonder why you have taken against me ?' he said, with a sweet, indulgent smile, which the other found exasperating. ' But perhaps we may get on better in the morning—I shall be willing to try.'

And then he went away with good-night adieux to his aunt and Philippa, which the one found delightful and the other resented unreasonably, as marking more sharply the lamentable difference between her nephew and her son.

Things did not go pleasantly at Rookhurst during the next few days. Sir Owen had insisted upon seeing his invalid grandson, in order, as he said, to judge for himself whether the improvement in his health, of which his mother spoke, were maintained; and Edward's sullen shrinking from his presence and accost, although the latter was not unkindly, excited his displeasure.

'It is easy to see,' he remarked to his daughter-in-law, 'in what creed you bring your children up, and yet I have not been so bad a friend to you and yours. Philippa runs away if she catches sight of me, and the little imp here looks as if he would like to fly at my throat. What sort of reception did you get, Bertie?'

'Oh, it was late, and he was ill and tired, and in that case temper doesn't count. I think I shall try and win him over with my fiddle.'

Mrs. Yorke looked at the speaker, and then dropped her eyes. The sight hurt her; for here was one in ample possession of all that her unhappy son lacked, and she had not magnanimity enough to forgive him. It was in vain that Gilbert did his best to please her; the very fact that he was in such favour with his grandfather that to please him needed no effort at all was a stone of stumbling and rock of offence to her, nor was she in any way mollified by his attentions to Philippa, since their natural effect was to excite an enthusiasm of liking that irritated her own jealousy.

But to the young girl, who had been kept too strictly in the shadow of her brother's affliction, this unexpected communion with health, youth, and vivacity was like a burst of sunshine. Gilbert had the power, which was simply the consequence of his own sincerity and naturalness, of setting everyone at ease with him; and Philippa, as she did the honours of the estate and neighbourhood, found her tongue loosened by his ready sympathy, and revealed her sorrows and aspirations in a way that she would have thought impossible a few days before.

It may be supposed that the confidences were not all on one side. Gilbert made her acquainted

with his lost mother and their life at Florence, till
the intensity of the girl's fellow-feeling checked the
passion of his reminiscences, and he followed up
these disclosures by the revelation of his musical
ambitions.

Then he told her about his uncle Martin's family,
and painted John Cartwright's merits in terms so
glowing that the boy would have laughed aloud
could he have heard himself thus Homerically
described, and Philippa would have been sorely
disappointed had she met him in the flesh. But
Gilbert Yorke saw everything he loved in a sort of
rainbow glory.

His talent as a violinist had been duly exhibited
to his new kinsfolk, Sir Owen himself taking a
certain reserved pride in the brilliancy of his gift;
but neither Mrs. Yorke nor her children were
susceptible of the spell of music, and Gilbert
saw, with a pang of acute disappointment—in
which not a particle of personal vanity mingled—
that his loveliest melodies, which set his own soul

on fire, or dissolved it into softness, produced no effect upon them.

Philippa looked at the musician with soft, admiring eyes that chafed his artist sense almost more than indifference itself; and her mother coldly admitted that ' No doubt he played very well for an amateur, and so young an one, but that, personally, she had never cared for the violin.'

One of these performances had taken place, at Gilbert's wish, in Edward's room; but the boy soon put an end to it by stopping his ears, and launching forth an angry protest.

' Leave off!' he cried; 'I cannot bear it! The thing speaks and cries. Leave off, I say!' and the outraged musician restored his fiddle to its case in almost the worst humour he ever remembered.

Sir Owen laughed delightedly. It always amused him to see anyone in a passion, and there was a gleam of anger in his grandson's eyes fiercer than he had supposed they could express; also he was

not at all displeased to find that the relations he
had disparaged, and Gilbert had been so eager
to know, were proving themselves almost as disagreeable as he had represented.

'We will get back to London, Bert,' he said;
'we are wasting ourselves here. Besides, it is
high time you had found a bear-leader, and were
started on your travels. You have three or four
years of hard work before you, worse luck; for
I should have liked nothing better than introducing
you into society, and seeing you make a figure in
it. Eh! what's wrong? The notion does not
please you !'

'I was thinking, if I had been allowed to follow
my calling, what those three or four years of down-
right hard work would have made me.'

He pressed the violin he was still holding against
his side, as if it had been a sentient thing, and
looked Sir Owen boldly in the face.

'Forgive me,' he added, reading there the angry
annoyance he had excited; 'I can't help fret-

ting over my good fortune. Society will never give me anything as good as what it takes away.'

It was this boldness, this absolute disregard of consequences, that gave Gilbert the advantage over his grandfather. He might mutter an oath, call him 'fool' and 'pleb.,' and work himself into a furious passion; but all this left matters precisely where they were before. Had Sir Owen turned the boy out of doors on the spot, he knew that he would have run back to Copplestone, joyful in the deliverance that put it in his power to carry out the ridiculous programme sketched in Mrs. Cartwright's letter, and with scarcely a regret for the brilliant prospects he had dropped.

On this occasion he let the matter pass with a contemptuous wave of the hand.

'The friction of the world will rub down this folly,' he remarked; 'it is the only mortar for a fool. May I ask if it will suit your convenience to leave Rookhurst to-morrow?'

'Of course—I am at your orders,' said Gilbert;
'only I was just going to beg for two days' leave of
absence.  Must we go to-morrow?'

'You have friends in the neighbourhood?' in-
quired the old man diplomatically.

Gilbert smiled.

'Yes; dear friends.'

Sir Owen shrugged his shoulders.

'Go if you like, but, remember, your furlough
lasts no longer than Thursday afternoon.  We do
not sit down to dinner without you.  Will you take
a horse or the dog-cart to the station?  You know,
I suppose, it is five miles off.'

'The dog-cart.  I am not used to ride, and it
would be a poor return for all your kindness to
make myself a laughing-stock to your grooms.'

'Good heavens!' ejaculated Sir Owen; and then
amazement held him dumb.  For a well-born
Yorke not to be able to ride—albeit a good seat on
horseback is difficult to acquire without the horse
—was a deficiency that seemed to partake equally

of misfortune and disgrace ; but the spark of humour in Gilbert's eyes, together with his delightful freedom from *mauraise honte,* mollified his disgust.

'For shame's sake, boy, keep your own secret !' he exclaimed. 'You shall have lessons as soon as you get back to town—twelve hours out of the twenty-four !'

# CHAPTER XV.

GILBERT, on getting out at the station at Copplestone, rushed off at once to his uncle's shop, sure of a cordial welcome, and he was in no sense disappointed. He had little difficulty in persuading Martin Cartwright to throw up business for the day and go home to Elm Lodge.

'But John will be at the college,' Gilbert suggested eagerly. 'Dear uncle, write a note to Dr. Fleming on the spot, asking for twenty-four hours' leave of absence—we must have a night together like old times—and send a messenger with it at once.'

This was done, not without a twinkle in Martin's

eye as he penned his petition, recognising Gilbert's anxiety to forestall possible opposition.

The heart of the elder man, always warm to his sister's son, grew warmer as the two, linked arm-in-arm, trod the well-known streets together, and the boy poured forth the animated recital of his experiences.

Martin Cartwright had felt Gilbert's absence acutely—it was a vital force dropped out of his life—and he took comfort therefore in the knowledge that what had cost him more than anyone knew had resulted at least in his nephew's gain. Looking at him critically, he found him improved —to this result, doubtless, a London tailor had largely contributed—but he seemed more robust, and to his natural charm of manner there was a something added of growing manliness and self-restraint.

Mrs. Cartwright, who had been sitting reading in the afternoon quiet of the house, was disturbed and surprised at the sound of their footsteps ; she had just put down her book, and had risen to leave the room to make inquiries when Martin and Gilbert entered together.

'Here, mother,' said the former cheerily, 'I have brought the truant home! You won't refuse to take the lad back again?'

For a moment she lost her self-possession. Gilbert, who was watching closely the effect of the words, saw that not only did she turn pale, but that a look of distressed appeal came into her beautiful eyes, as if against a blow she could neither bear nor understand.

She struggled to speak, but seemed at a loss for the fitting words. This involuntary proof of her aversion gave him a pang deeper than she had ever inflicted before. He bit his lip in sharp vexation.

'Don't be frightened, aunt!' he said, in a curious, constrained voice; 'Uncle Martin is only joking—I have my grandfather's leave to come and see you and John, but I go back to-morrow. With

your leave,' he added, ' I will run upstairs and see
if my old room is looking as it used;' and without
heeding her hand, outstretched to restrain him, he
turned and made good his escape. He had seen
the burning glow of shame cover her face and the
angry light in his uncle's eyes, and he knew that
one of the rare occasions had come when the husband ventured to reprove the wife, and that he was
the cause.

He sat down in the old rocking-chair, which
stood precisely at the same angle to the table as
on the day he had first seen it, and, swaying gently
backwards and forwards, brooded almost bitterly
over the incident, so trifling but so significant.

' After all,' he said to himself, ' I am only a
waif and stray. No one loves me. I have no
imperative claim on any human being. Sir Owen
Yorke and Aunt Cartwright are both equally free
to turn me out of doors at a moment's notice, and
she would have the best inclination in the world
to do it. Why does she hate me so?'

His mind fell back sorrowfully upon his mother, and upon all the unmatched love and tender sympathy that were buried in her grave, but this grief was a hopeless one, and he put it from him with a sigh. It was better to think of possibilities still open to him—of the bright, imperious girl who had been his friend and comrade in Florence, who had risked so much to tell him how her warm heart ached for his loss, and beat in tune with his now thwarted ambition. Would she have heard of the sudden change in his fortunes, and would the news seem to her good or bad, seeing she was almost as passionate a musician as himself? Yet it must be good if it brought them nearer; at her dear feet he was even prepared to deposit the sacrifice of his hopes.

It seemed as if he had sat alone a long time, when the sound of familiar footsteps roused him at once; the door opened as he sprang to meet them, and the next moment he had seized John's hand, dragged him across the floor, and thrust him down into the depths of the easy-chair, taking his familiar perch on the arm, and flinging his own about his neck.

It was proof of an unusual strain of feeling that for a moment or two neither of them spoke. Then John looked up.

'I did not expect this. The doctor was so kind; he let me go at once, and sent his love to you.'

His eyes softened as he gazed at the other.

'I suppose you are pretty safe to be loved, Gilbert, wherever you go?'

'Don't look like it, Jack; your mother hates me like—sin, shall we say? and my aunt Yorke loves me little better. But never mind all that! I want to hear about yourself—the college, the doctor, the sort of life, and whether you are happier there than at home? Yes, Jack, you are! There is a gladness in your eyes; you don't pucker your brows so much, and I believe you are taller.'

' Since we parted, six weeks ago ?'

'Ay, man ! six hours will do it in some cases, when the yoke is off, and the back straightened and the head erect. Jack, you are looking different —as if your soul had more room to move—you are not fretting, old fellow !'

Jack smiled. 'I am working very hard, which helps to keep trouble down, and — Dr. Fleming seems to understand me, and that cheers me up. Still, I have my worries, though some things run pretty straight; if I were at home I should miss you more, I think, than I could bear. But time is short; tell me about yourself. You get on with Sir Owen Yorke ?'

So the lads sat and talked in the gathering dusk, and again late at night before John turned into his own bed. He was to go back to the college the next morning after breakfast, and Gilbert was going with him to pay his respects to Dr. Fleming, and give in his report of himself before returning to Rookhurst. Each knew that they might not meet again for years, and both, in the abrupt in-articulate English fashion, renewed their pledge of friendship.

Among other last words Gilbert said shyly :

'Margery Denison will be at home long before I shall, Jack. You must find out all about her, and send me word.'

It had been on John's tongue to say, 'How will that be possible?' but he looked into Gilbert's face, and held his peace, accepting the difficulty as part of the contract.

The next morning, a few minutes before it was time for the lads to depart, Mrs. Cartwright called Gilbert into a room alone.

'I wanted to speak to you by yourself,' she said, with her grave smile, 'because I think a mother is never bound to humiliate herself before her son, and I want you to forgive me, Gilbert, for what seemed yesterday like cruelty and hardness of heart. It was not really so—but you would not understand. I am not hard towards you, as you

think; though you have done me an injury you
can never repair.'

'I!'

'None the less of an injury because it was an
involuntary one—perhaps so much the more.   But
I wish you well, and I want to say a few words of
warning to you before we part, which if I did not
say, it would weigh on my conscience as a sin.
Can you bear them?'

'I would bear a great deal from John's mother.'

Her face flushed; but the answer helped her to
fulfil her duty.

'Circumstances have changed with you,' she
began, 'and in my view not for the better.
Poverty and disappointment are harsh com-
panions; but they help to keep a young man of
your temper from going astray; what measure of
worth is in you will not stand the severe ordeal
of worldly prosperity.   I hear you are going
abroad almost as your own master, and with the
openly professed purpose of getting out of life all

the personal enjoyment you can. It seems to me right to warn you that so long as this is your aim you will lose not only what you expect to find, but everything else that exalts a human creature above the brutes who are irresponsible, and makes him in his poor degree acceptable to God.'

She stopped, her voice trembling a little with the strength of her feelings.

Gilbert did not answer; he was neither impressed nor irritated.

A sentiment of indulgent tolerance was what his aunt's stern pietism excited in his mind. She in her turn, looking at his face, was moved to anger.

'My words are of no account?' she said; 'you reject my warning.'

'It has been given me without option of rejection. Simply I do not understand what you mean. What is it I ought to do and leave undone?' He smiled slightly, then added, 'I have never thought much of myself.'

'If I explain, you will not hear; but I will try

and explain. You are self-deceived in thinking you have a low opinion of yourself—you are full of pride and presumption. I would have you first of all pray to God to convince you of the sin of which you have no knowledge. Without this you grope in the dark, and cannot see the bearings of the spiritual life. Then I would have you take up the yoke of humility and self-denial, following, though at an awful distance, the example of Him whom even the natural man adores. It will lead you, Gilbert, into that straight path which you have never trod nor wished to tread, for it lies over the neck of natural desire.'

Her face lighted up, and for a moment she looked at him tenderly.

'Will you try?' she said softly.

'Isn't it possible to please God and others and self as well? Doesn't it depend a little upon what one's "natural desire" is?'

'Ah!' she cried sharply, 'that is the devil's own snare—nature has done so much there is no room for grace! Poor boy! When the time comes, as come it will, that this pretty conceit of yourself crumbles into ashes, you will taste a humiliation much more bitter than that to which I have vainly exhorted you. But I have done.'

' At least you will wish me well ?' he asked.

' I wish everybody well,' she replied; ' but such wishes are of poor account. In your case I will wish you what you least wish for yourself.'

' I will accept your good wishes according to your own interpretation, and be grateful, only—let us part friends. You were very good to me about Leipzig.'

He sighed. She looked at him attentively, and then re-echoed his sigh.

This gave him courage; he went on like one who has taken a sudden resolution.

' Dare I say one word of warning on my side ? You know that I love John very dearly—as long as I live I shall never forget how good he was to me when I first came here, miserable and a stranger. I know — forgive me — that you love him almost as well as my mother loved me. I should like to beg you to let him know it, too.'

'*Almost* as well!' she repeated scornfully.

She tried to gather herself up to sternness and self-repression, but the effort failed. Gilbert saw her proud lip quiver, and tears dim her eyes. Then he caught her hand in both his and kissed it.

'I will love you for ever!' he cried, in his eager, passionate way, 'whatever you may think of me, if only you will comfort Jack when I am gone away.'

And so they parted.

# PART II.

# CHAPTER I.

WHEN Margery Denison came up to town from her Yorkshire solitude to make her curtsy to her Queen, and pass her first London season, under the chaperonage of a distant kinswoman, who had undertaken the office from a strong sense of family obligation, all the world expected that she would mend her fortunes by a splendid match.

But Miss Denison returned home without being engaged. Indeed, amongst her warmest and dearest friends it was whispered she had not even received any offer of marriage, and the girl never contradicted the report.

The experiment was repeated under the same

protection a second season, and with the same
result ; but on this occasion a reason was assigned.
Young Gilbert Yorke, the grandson of the notorious
old worldling, Sir Owen Yorke, was in town also,
and in such constant attendance upon Miss Denison that the fact of their engagement was widely
circulated and believed.    It was so implicitly
believed by Viscount Thimberley, who had been
hesitating ever since his first introduction to
Margery whether he should lay his coronet at her
feet, and intreat her to forget the disparity between
one-and-twenty and fifty years in consideration of
his rent-roll and splendid constitution, that he left
town without putting his fortune to the touch.

'I do not care about being a rejected suitor,' he
said confidentially to the sister who presided over
his bachelor establishments, the first evening after
his return to that charming little seat in Surrey
which is the pride and envy of half the county.

He was sitting near the open window, watching
the sun set gorgeously behind the elm-tops, where

he and his forefathers had watched the same spectacle for generations, with his cigar between his fingers and a cup of black coffee by his side.

'I saw that I had not a chance; the fellow is ridiculously young in all the meanings of the word, with a tongue as glib as an Irish Nationalist, and a prodigious knack with the fiddle. Miss Denison is music-mad herself.'

'And you,' said the lady, smiling — she was naturally disposed to bear her brother's disappointment with equanimity—'are not able to tell one tune from another. I remember that at the last concert we were at you stood up for "God save the Queen" when the band had just led off a series of Scotch airs with "Scots, wha hae!" I think it is a good thing you have not married the girl. Besides, she has not a penny!'

'Neither has young Yorke, beyond what his grandfather allows him. All the world knows that Margery Denison is bound to marry money.'

He replaced his cigar and smoked meditatively,

his sister adding, with a touch of female diplomacy :

‘ In that case, my dear Thimberley, you have still
a chance.  No doubt the market will be open for
you another season.’

The market was open, for Margery was again in
town in the following spring, still ‘on her promotion,’ as the fresh young *débutantes* delighted to
whisper ; but their freshness failed in the competi-
tion with her.

Society was quite of one mind that she was more
attractive and brilliant than ever.  Had she had a
fortune at her back she could not have borne herself with more pride of independence.  If suitors
came, they came unsolicited and unwelcomed,
fascinated either by the spell of her beauty, of her
superb indifference, or of her racy speech, in which
there was an odd mixture of ardour, keenness and
cynicism.

To dance with Margery Denison was, so far as it
went, a liberal education for any man ; but when

Gilbert Yorke was her partner, so perfect was the harmony of poise and sense that the waltz, instead of being a mere sensuous gratification, was spiritualized to the height of an artistic rapture.

One night near the close of the season, at a ball given by the French Ambassador, Margery Denison and Gilbert Yorke had danced together with unusual frequency and delight, even in spite of the young lady's accusing conscience and the protests of her chaperon.

' I have done wrong,' she said to him at last, ' and I want to confess and explain. Find some quiet corner where we can talk ;' and Gilbert had found such a corner—palm-leaved and rose-perfumed, in the deep embrasure of a window—and was sitting beside her as she slowly fanned herself, waiting for her to speak, with every pulse beating with excitement.

' My excuse for behaving as I have done to-night,' she began, ' is that it was my last chance. I go home to-morrow, and Mrs. Anstruther washes her hands of me for ever. I think she is justified, for I cannot deny that I have had my chances and thrown them away; but she is making things very hard for me by exasperating my father against me. You will own that was hardly necessary.'

'And why do you let such chances go? So long as you do this I shall hope, even though you forbid me to hope. I could not live otherwise.'

She smiled, her eyes glancing over his face and figure.

'I don't see a sign of discouragement in dress or aspect! You think I am necessary to you, but that is a mistake, the result of habit and old association. We are fond of each other, I allow, as comrades and friends, but it would suit neither of us to pass life together. Trouble has made my vision clear.' Her face hardened a little as she spoke.

'I am sorry for my father,' she went on, 'and would have met his wishes if I could. Indeed, I should have been guilty of a fraud if I had come to town for three successive seasons with any other intention. Like all women who keep the nature God gave them, I love wealth and ease and distinction, but I must not buy them too dear—with my soul as well as my body. My hope was I might meet with some man who was able to give me these, and for whom I could entertain a decent affection. It was a wild hope, no doubt, and I did not fail to point that out to my friends; so if they persisted in the belief that I should be tempted to take the one without the other, the fault is not mine. Lord Thimberley—there is no indelicacy in speaking to my friend of what he knows—is a kind, worthy man, and has shown great disinterestedness; but he is two years older than my father, and we have not an idea or interest in common. As a wife under those conditions I would not trust myself.'

'Can I help you in any way?' he asked.

She hesitated. 'Yes, if I may put your loyalty

to the test. You will be at Rookhurst sooner or
later. I ask you not to come to The Chace. If
my father knew—of this—he would draw false
conclusions, and make things still more unplea-
sant.'

'If your father knew—of what?' asked Gilbert,
leaning forward to look into her face. 'Margery,
you allow that you love me!'

Possibly it was the inflection of his voice, or the
expression of his face, that touched her; but, be
that as it may, a wave of colour swept over her
face and neck, and brought the blood surging to
Gilbert's heart. But he controlled himself, being
as much on guard as a knight of old watching his
armour. Besides, he detected at once the look of
acute annoyance that followed—how pale she
grew, and with what hurt dignity she raised her
head.

'Yes, I have allowed that for years,' she said,
'and repeated it again to-night. Let me repeat,
too, what I have been compelled also to say before

—that it would be easier to turn dislike or indifference into the feeling you desire than the sort of affection which I have for you.'

The nineteenth-century lover does not often turn pale under discussions of the tender passion, but Gilbert grew unquestionably paler. Margery had spoken not only with energy, but also with bitterness.

'You force me to appear odious,' she said, speaking rapidly and in a low tone; 'but, in fact, I am your best friend. My father would not resent an engagement between us more stringently than would Sir Owen Yorke. Believe me, he would cut you off with a penny; and, pardon me, you have become used to the spending of a good many. It is an art soon acquired, I perceive. I have no personal experience to fall back upon, but you have taken kindly to it.'

She got up and looked about her, as if in search of her chaperon, her motive being to look anywhere rather than at her silent companion; but her

impulsive kindness mastered her, and she sat down
again.

'It is of no use to be angry with a girl so miserable as I am,' she said, in the same low, hurried
tone, and touching his arm, as if in deprecation.
' I hate to complain, but you know to what a home
I am going back and the prospect that life holds
out to me.  If you would lighten it a little, be on
your guard not to excite my father's suspicions.
That is why I dared to ask you not to come to The
Chace.'

' I will not come.'

' Thanks ; but I shall long for you !'

He smiled, for the thought passed through his
mind that a woman's tender mercies were cruel,
but he did not express it.

Margery, however, read him like a book.

' You are right,' she said, blushing deeply, ' and
my selfishness is hateful.  My poor excuse is that
I have had no training in nobleness.  You had a
mother that might have spiritualized a clod, and

instead of a clod to work on, she had the finest, purest clay that was ever quickened by the vital spark. There, I see Mrs. Anstruther! Take me to her, and then say good-night and good-bye to both of us.'

This dialogue had taken place some five years later than when we dropped the thread of a story that was spun so closely over the record of a few months. The transition point in many lives was marked out when Martin Cartwright walked home to his house through the November fog, with his dead sister's letter in his pocket.

There are periods when life lingers to stamp a direct impress on every day and hour, and others when it marks its course by leaps and bounds, leaving scarce a trace behind.

During those few months John Cartwright had received two impressions, that he was to carry to the grave with him; one the love, sudden as passion itself, excited by the unknown kinsman who brought into his dreary home the strange charm of sweetness and ardour, vivified by the touch of genius; the other a passion also, but disallowed and kept under.

Margery Denison had captured, in utter unconsciousness, the locked soul of the awkward, reticent lad, from the first moment when he saw her brilliant, animated face, and heard her voice as she leaned from the carriage to greet Gilbert Yorke, with eager, friendly hands. A little later he had seen her again, disguised in a hideous mackintosh, which only served to throw into relief the beauty of the fresh, rain-dewed face, vivid with ardent welcome once more for Gilbert Yorke.

From that time till the present he had been, unknown to herself, associated with Margery. Gilbert had left him a charge to keep, and John, for his sake, overcame his natural reluctance, and ceaselessly sought for such news of her as could filter through the ordinary channels of gossip without offending his delicate sense of propriety, in order that he might transmit them to his friend.

He knew when her holidays began and ended, and when the term of school-life was fulfilled; and he even planned to find occasions of meeting her in her carriage or on foot, so that he might lift a furtive glance to her sweet face, and remark whether it were smiling or sad.

And so the slow years had run on.

Four of them had been passed in the deep seclusion of Wesley College, where, amongst many worthy competitors, John Cartwright was the ripest scholar and best-loved inmate. Unhappily the death of Dr. Fleming occurred in the second year of his residence, and his successor was a man of a different spirit. Where the one had seen the sunshine of the Divine Fatherhood, the other walked in the shadow of the Divine judgment; the first had opened to the boys every avenue of legitimate delight, not degrading the senses, but ennobling them; the last shut the door against all the amenities of life, reducing it to a sort of barrack-ground, where the recruits were to be rigidly drilled for their future warfare against the world, the flesh, and the devil.

Unfortunately, again, this happened to be a period of dissension and reorganization in the Connexion, and the points of creed and discipline involved seemed of such supreme importance to the zealous Doctor that he gave them a prominence both in his private and public teaching which dwarfed all broader issues. The question seemed less that his pupils should feel and do right than that they should grasp the interests at stake, and be prepared to defend them.

He did not appear to have recognised the elementary truth that a selfish and ignoble life is quite compatible with a flawless orthodoxy.

The religious life, which Dr. Fleming's nurture had opened before John Cartwright, as a divine organism capable of unlimited development, closed again and shut up his soul as within prison bars.

His experiences were at this time severe. He seemed to withdraw into himself, keeping former

companionships at arm's-length ; and while working at his books with a dogged persistency that
secured the success to which he was indifferent,
he was secretly engaged in weighing the insoluble
problems of his professed faith in an agony of
solicitude.

All this time—and it lasted long—he shrank from
his mother's eye as a criminal undetected. He
would almost as soon have plunged a knife into her
bosom as have told her the truth ; and as she
watched him with a speechless anxiety, he did his
best to escape from her society. There were times
when she would question him about his bodily
health with an apprehension so intense that it con-
sumed her strange reserve, and let the secret tenderness appear. Once or twice the temptation
almost mastered him to fall at her knees and pour
out his burdened heart with his head hidden in her
lap ; but he never yielded—from the grievous doubt
how such a confession would be received.

Probably his health would have given way under

the strain had he been deprived of all outlet; but there was his friend and cousin, Gilbert Yorke.

In an odd sort of way the stern and conscientious youth made of this bright and gay spirit his Father Confessor, writing to him every week, not of outside matters, which were few enough, but of the inward revolt and turmoil of his soul. Happily, the letters did not run to great length. John Cartwright had a splendid gift of condensation, and Gilbert Yorke not only read them as a point of conscience, but with that sympathetic insight which is the last, best gift of the imaginative faculty.

He was at this time at Leipzig, under the care of the excellent tutor his grandfather's perspicacity had provided for him, and dividing his time between the University, where his natural aptitudes balanced a little his indifference to scholarship, and the Conservatoire, where his mixed talent and devotion were such as to make him the spoilt child of every professor.

But full as his days were—for he took his share

of the fun and folly of the student-life by which he
was surrounded—very few of John's letters waited
long for an answer; and if his own lacked authority
and wisdom, they were imbued with the fellow-feeling which their recipient stood most in need of,
and sometimes, with the unconscious truth of intui-
tion, words were said or ideas suggested that had a
certain power of healing in them.

But in due course of time, on the details of which
it is not our purpose to dwell, John Cartwright's
soul struggled forth from its eclipse of faith. It
would have been a moral impossibility for such as
he to have drifted into infidelity, as great as the
natural impossibility for a tree to survive which the
axe has severed from the root. Whether he had
imbibed it with his mother's milk, or even before he
awoke to conscious existence, the idea of a Supreme
Being, bound to His creatures, if not by golden
chains, at least by irrefragable ties of connection,
was part and parcel of his heart and brain.

To stand, orphaned of God, in a vacant universe,

robbed of the Divine imperative of duty, and the obligation of responsibility, would have been a bereavement so poignant and absolute that neither his strength of body nor mind would have been able to sustain it. It is written, ' He that doeth the Will of God shall know of His doctrine '; and henceforth it was John Cartwright's resolution to know no will of his own.

It was in this temper that he took his vows and entered on his ministry.

# CHAPTER II.

## AN EPISODE.

Once during Gilbert Yorke's residence at Leipzig the friends met.

It happened in this way. The summer vacation of both the young men corresponded fairly in point of time, and Martin Cartwright, seriously concerned at the drooping state of his son's spirits, if not of his health, suggested that he should try the effect of foreign travel.

He was at liberty to join his cousin at Leipzig, share the supervision of his tutor, and, if agreeable to all three, they could make a short tour in France and Italy; he was prepared to be paymaster for the party.

It was one of those few occasions when the good man did not take his wife into counsel until all his arrangements were made, and he silenced her strenuous opposition by the emphatic assertion:

' John must be roused!'

John Cartwright came back effectually roused. The mere change of scene and the new excitement of travel stimulated his sluggish organs and quickened the flow of his blood. He had been born and bred in Copplestone, and had seen nothing outside it but one or two places on the Yorkshire coast. For the first time he stood in the midst of great cities, and heard not only the multitudinous hum of complex human life, but the ground-swell which historic ages leave behind them; for the first time he got a glimpse of the magnitude of Art—a word that hitherto had meant very little to him— and perceived how pitiful man's heritage would have been if no Stones had been reared in Venice, no canvas painted by immortal hands in Rome and Florence, nor the divine Ideal of humanity released from the marble block that bound it, in ancient Greece. Nor was it perhaps the least of his privileges that for the first time his eyes drank in the unadulterated sunshine as it streamed over the fathomless blue water of the Maggiore Lake.

All this was very good for John, but better still was the society of his cousin and his cousin's tutor. The latter was a pleasant gentleman, a good scholar and a moderate Churchman, and in the ordinary flow of daily intercourse it sometimes happened that talk fell into deeper channels, and that the close texture and earnestness of John's mind were permeated and relaxed by contact with a wider experience and a more benign intelligence.

For the rest, the ties of friendship were strengthened; if his cousin failed to meet some of the moral demands of his spirit, he satisfied him on all other points. It was still a pleasure to him, patiently conscious of his own deficiencies, to watch Gilbert, to whom every change of circumstance or experience seemed to develop some new charm

without robbing him of the old. There was also
Gilbert's musical genius to be taken into account,
which, in John's opinion, separated him from the
rest of the world as something unique and unap-
proachable.

And, indeed, the young man had such a fine gift
that it did seem an infinite pity that he was not
going to dedicate his life to his Art.

He had of course improved beyond John's capacity of estimate, and when he saw the intense pleasure his performance gave him, Gilbert was anxious
to drag his cousin to opera and concert room in order
to open his ears still wider, and to give him some
more perfect notion of that phantom world of
divinely ordinated sound which was to himself the
central point of life. But here John stood resolute.

'First,' he said, 'my mother objects to these
places of amusement; secondly, I know quite well
that I am so weak that I should not be able to
stand up against the effects of what you describe.'

'Why, what would happen?' asked Gilbert, laughing.

'A general melting away of all sense of duty and responsibility, leaving nothing behind but a mad craving to go on listening so long as I had ears to hear. I feel it with your fiddle, Gilbert, and you will own this would scarcely do for a Methodist parson.'

'And you will still be that?'

'Please God and my masters, I will; but that remains to be seen.'

# CHAPTER III.

## THE DEAD HAND.

WHEN Gilbert had reached twenty-three years of age Sir Owen Yorke congratulated himself on the success of his grandson's training.

He had passed through his University course both in Germany and at Oxford: not, indeed, with any brilliancy as scholar or prizeman, but with just that degree of distinction which becomes a gentleman, and his social success had been considerable.

After he had taken his degree, Sir Owen encouraged him to taste the full delights of a London season, exerting himself to introduce him to all the 'smart' and influential people of his own acquaintance, and being quite ignorant that Gilbert's intense enjoyment of his privileges depended upon the fact that he either met or hoped to meet Margery Denison at the great houses to which each had the *entrée.*

The autumn was spent at Rookhurst, Sir Owen laying claim to his grandson's companionship and attendance, as his failing health disinclined him for any further exertion in the pursuit of pleasure, either on his own behalf or Gilbert's.

'You owe me a great deal,' the old man said to the young one, 'and I expect to be paid back a little. Suppose you try to make yourself as agreeable to me as I am told you do to other people.'

Gilbert responded loyally to the appeal, and proved a delightful companion, accommodating himself to the humours of the querulous and exacting invalid with that natural sweetness of temper which makes it an open question in ethics whether his merit were less or more because it cost him so little.

Then his was the blessed possession of a superb

hobby, and one to which he had not much difficulty in reconciling his grandfather.

Sir Owen was a man of considerable musical discernment, and was able to appreciate and enjoy in moderation Gilbert's violin, and the musician himself had tact and discretion enough never to weary him.

But Sir Owen went early to bed, and then—shut up in his own chamber in the square tower above the gateway, out of earshot of the household—Gilbert's hours of pure rapture set in.

He was now a skilled, almost a consummate, musician, and Sir Owen's kindness had provided him with an instrument as good as trained discernment could discover, while his ardour was so pure and sincere as to be able to dispense with an audience. Whether such periods of refined self-indulgence were altogether salutary may be doubted.

Music, of however high an order, has the inevitable tendency, through exalting the senses and stimulating the imagination, to plunge the spirit of a man into that condition of indefinite desire and inexplicable yearning which drains the sap from resolution and endeavour.

It was in such hours as these that Gilbert fed his passion for Margery Denison, endowing it and her and himself with a golden glamour that had its rise undoubtedly in his constitutional fidelity, but which took its most exquisite tints from the medium through which he contemplated it.

He had already had the opportunity of meeting her in town, of which he had made all the use that a lover could who was at once patient and devoted, and he had gone to The Chace to pay his respects to the family once or twice since his return to Rookhurst, undismayed by the coldness of his reception. That he should meet her in town again in the spring was the base on which all his plans and hopes for the coming season were fixed.

Sir Owen was anxious, if his health permitted,

to be in London in April. He had a great desire
(not shared by his grandson) to get him the post
of *attaché* to some European embassy, and he
believed himself to have influence with our
Ambassador at Vienna, who was expected to be
in town on urgent private affairs about that date.

'I rely, Bert,' he said, 'not on your possession
of any special endowment of brains, but on your
good looks and good manners—your knowledge of
the modern tongues, too, ought to stand you in
some stead; and, then, you are an excellent
dancer. You will find that useful, though the
fiddle may prove a nuisance.'

Sir Owen rallied sufficiently to carry out his
programme, and take his grandson up to town
with him; but to his disappointment the Ambassador delayed his coming. It was not such to
Gilbert himself. Margery was in town, as we
have described, for her last season, and it was
during this time that the incidents occurred which
we have related earlier. Owing to her father's

peremptory orders, based on her rejection of Lord Thimberley's offer of marriage, she had gone back to her Yorkshire home before Sir Hugh Dalrymple made his appearance in London.

When he did arrive, however, all went smoothly. He was about to enjoy a well-earned holiday, and was in the best of spirits. Sir Owen had no occasion to recall to his mind the circumstances on which he grounded his claims to the great man's favour—namely, a certain obligation which he had conferred upon the Ambassador in his youth. The latter was at that time a distinguished but impecunious youngster, and Sir Owen himself a wealthy and experienced man of the world. It had not cost the one much personal risk, and the other accepted it as a favour never to be fully discharged. Sir Hugh Dalrymple was the first to allude to it, and to express his regret that since that time he had found no way of marking his gratitude except by empty words.

Nothing could have been more opportune. Gilbert was presented, and the favour asked and granted. Six weeks later the young man left London in the suite of an Ambassador whose favour was the title-deed of personal distinction, for it was never lightly won nor lightly lost.

Sir Owen, in a thoroughly complacent frame of mind, went down to Dover to see his grandson off, in spite of a previous passage of arms on account of Gilbert's having carried out his stubborn determination not to leave England without going to bid his cousin, John Cartwright, good-bye.

His pledge to Margery was binding; but he wrote to tell her of his destination; and he besought her, not in vain, to meet him once more in the Iddersleigh meadows, and to wish him 'God speed.'

He was not so cheerful as his grandfather, as they stood on the deck of the steamer exchanging their farewells. Sir Owen had made arrangements with his bankers for placing a really munificent allowance to the young man's credit, and his last words were, 'I object to your running into debt, and you will have no excuse for doing so; but my wish is that you should be able to take the position of my grandson and probable heir. 'Pon my soul, you are a lucky dog! Vienna is the crown of the civilized world. You will rub off there the last stain of your provincialism.'

On his homeward way to Rookhurst, the old baronet stopped to pay a short visit to his daughter-in-law at her pretty little place in Kent. He had a cynical pleasure in telling her about his other grandson's successes, for which he, is not to be forgiven. Besides, he liked to take, as he expressed it, periodical stock of the condition of Edward Yorke, who still persisted in living on in spite of the conclusive advantages to be derived from his decease. He found things curiously the same as when he had last seen them, except that they were all just so many years older.

The invalid, who appeared to be neither better

nor worse, still lay on his couch and ruled the household from it with, in a sense, a whip of scorpions. Mrs. Yorke looked more aged than the years alone would have made her, and her temper, as Philippa could have borne witness, was sharper and more irritable.

The girl herself—but we will hear Sir Owen on this point.

'Why, Bella, I declare the child has positively grown! If she were better dressed and in better health—what a pity you cannot exchange complexions!—she would be almost presentable. She has finer eyes even than her mother. By-and-by we shall be obliged to see what we can do for her.'

'By - and - by!' repeated Mrs. Yorke acidly. 'Philippa is now twenty-one; may I ask what appears to you the proper age for a girl to go into society?'

'Precisely at the age that commends itself to her mother—it is evident that period has not arrived. I shall have to find a chaperon for my grand - daughter myself next season. Philippa, my dear, look to me—you shall have a better chance in the world than you have reason to expect.'

But when next season opened, Sir Owen was ailing too much to think of any interest so remote as Philippa Yorke—at least, in the way that he had promised. He refused to have his grandson sent for, believing that he should rally again, as he had so often done before. But this was not to be; life, fortified by a constitution of iron, was spun out to its last filament. He was found dead in his bed one fine May morning when his valet entered the room at the usual hour, with every appearance of having passed away peacefully in his sleep.

His will had been made soon after Gilbert's departure for Vienna, and placed in the hands of Mr. Percival, the old family solicitor, head of the firm Percival and Kenyon, York, with the instructions that it was to be read aloud immediately

after the funeral to whatever relatives and friends
might be in attendance.

The testator had it in his power to alienate
every acre and shilling he possessed from the man
who was to succeed to the empty title—Edward
Yorke, the son of Sir Owen's eldest son; and he
exercised that power.

With the exception of legacies to his servants,
which did not err on the side of liberality, and one
of five thousand pounds to his daughter-in-law, all
that Sir Owen possessed in land or personalty was
bequeathed to his grandson, Gilbert Yorke.

The bequest, however, was not absolute.  Some
desire to redress the balance of injustice had probably stirred the old man's conscience, and induced him to base the condition of inheritance
upon Gilbert's marriage with his first cousin,
Philippa Yorke, within a year of the testator's
death.

In default of compliance on the man's side,
the estate devolved on a distant kinsman, with

an allowance of three hundred a year to the recusant, and five hundred a year to the girl he rejected.

Curiously enough, no provision had been made to meet the contingency of Philippa's refusal to marry Gilbert Yorke.

The lawyer had duly pointed out the absence of this provision, but his client had refused to recognise it. The young man, he declared, was irresistible, and the girl already over head and ears in love with him. Besides, he objected to put on record his belief in a woman's capacity to renounce a fortune. The result was obvious as the will stood.

The will was read in full conclave, after the due performance of somewhat ceremonious obsequies. Sir Owen Yorke was laid to rest with his fathers in the vault beneath the chancel of the old parish church, with a large gathering of assistant clergy and an elaborate choral service, according to his own written instructions.

The heir was not present at either ceremony, being struck down by typhoid fever, and lying sick at the house of the English Ambassador in the Land Strasse, Vienna.

# CHAPTER IV.

## FATHER AND DAUGHTER.

It was four o'clock in the afternoon of Midsummer Day, and the season was in harmony with the calendar. The sky was without a cloud, and the atmosphere seemed to palpitate with light and heat.

Cyril Denison sat in a deep-cushioned chair in the library of The Chace, and gazed wearily at the scene outside.

The limes and chestnuts, which formed one of the most effective features of the pleasure-grounds surrounding the house, were in full beauty—every leaf and blossom at the point of perfect development, and yet retaining the tender freshness of spring. The air was so still that not a leaf stirred; and the shadows upon the grass were as motionless as if carved in stone. Even the birds were silent, except at intervals the drowsy coo of a wood-pigeon from a distant plantation, murmuring to herself in the depth of her content.

So far the outlook was beautiful; but of the beauty Cyril Denison saw little or nothing. His eyes were fixed on the flaws in the picture. The small garden immediately round the house was in fair order, but he was looking beyond, towards neglected lawns, untrimmed borders, and straggling flower-beds. The 'pleasaunce' of The Chace had been planned for full coffers and a staff of gardeners, and quite exceeded the means at the disposal of the one man and boy which were all the present reduced establishment supplied.

Weeds sprang up at intervals through all the length of the broad gravel walks that wound hither and thither, following the picturesque undulations of the ground; and the gravel itself was gray and

sunken. In one once-charming corner of the
demesne there had been a large fish-pond; but the
reservoir had long been empty, the marble parapet
was chipped and broken, and a great willow which
had hung over the brink, as if to see its own reflection, was dead from drought, and its ungainly
branches stood out stark against the deep-blue
sky. The rustic bench beside it required the
carpenter's hammer and nails; and the long green
'ride,' as it was called, which stretched for a
quarter of a mile from this point to the park
beyond, and the sward of which in other days had
looked like a strip of velvet, was now lush with
flowering grasses and wild clover.

There is perhaps something in the decadence
and neglect of a house meant for wealth and
pleasure more depressing than the sight of abject
poverty itself. The force of contrast accentuates
the misfortune, and there is an instinctive impression that good birth and fine feeling go together—an
impression that must not be mistaken for a truth.

Cyril Denison surveyed these evidences of his low estate with a bitterness that never seemed to grow less, adding to what he saw the knowledge of what was out of sight, and to this, again, the perpetual revolt of his spirit, not only against the condition of things, but against the physical misery he was called upon to endure. Trouble and pain, whether of body or mind, leave no man where they find him; if they do not purify and exalt, they exasperate and degrade.

In the world beyond his broken park-pales, every pleasure of sense, from the desire of the eye and of the ear, trained to nicest discernment, down to the mere unbridled pride of life, were, at that very hour, in fullest swing and exercise; while he, more susceptible of enjoyment than one man in a thousand, was cut off from his natural inheritance.

At all points he had been beaten and baffled by fate—thwarted or disappointed in every undertaking to which he had laid his hand, or been fool enough to trust his heart—hampered and shut in by poverty before he had half drained the wine of life; and yet even poverty was not the worst. Even as the thought pressed upon him a spasm of pain made his frame quiver, and whitened his lips.

It was not a happy moment for the door to open and his daughter to come in; he had heard her before she entered trilling the air, 'Come, ever-smiling Liberty,' in her delicious voice, and his face had darkened as he listened. It was not because he was insensible to the charm of her song, or disparaged her graces any more than her gifts, but because, being thus endowed for the market of the world, she had returned empty.

Add to this that health and energy, lightness of heart and liberty of action, were, if not an offence to Mr. Denison, at least the cause of intense irritation.

He looked up as she came nearer, and, having looked, he closed his eyes, as if the sight were disagreeable.

Margery was at this time twenty-two years old,

with every grace and charm fulfilled which her
delightful girlhood had promised; she was rather a
goddess than a sylph, being tall and erect, with
finely proportioned length of limb, and a poise of
the head upon the beautiful neck and shoulders
which looked like pride, but was not. She was
also in possession of such perfect and harmonious
health that her aspect suggested nothing so much
as the idea of immortal youth.

She wore a white gown, with a bunch of yellow
roses at the throat, and the heat of the weather
had made her a little pale, but colour was no
necessary adjunct to the beauty of her face. Her
expression, which had been bright and gay when
she entered, changed to seriousness as her eyes fell
on her father, for the hard times under which Cyril
Denison groaned were not unshared by his daughter.
One could perceive that there was something
anxious and tentative in her speech and movements.

She took a seat on a couch near him, and looked,

as he was looking, out of the open window, not speaking for a moment or two. Then she said, in a low, caressing voice:

'Do you like that position best, dad? From the other window we see nothing but a lovely corner of the park, and smell the roses in the home garden. Let me move your chair!'

He shook his head impatiently.

'I am neither a woman nor a fool,' he said, 'to forget a thing because it is not before my eyes. You had better go away, Madge; I am in the clutch of my enemy—you can do me no good.'

'Oh that I could—just take turns with you in your pain!'

She got up and knelt beside his chair, passing her arm behind it, and leaning her head against his shoulder. The sun smote her bowed head, and turned the bronze to gold; the perfume of the roses she wore and the tender pressure of the hand which had fallen across his knee touched Mr. Denison's perceptions acutely. Besides, her whole attitude,

as well as the tones of her voice, expressed the
most intimate sympathy.

'Get up!' he said, in a stifled voice. 'You might
know by this time how little value I set on idle professions of love and duty. When it was in your
power to help me, you refused.'

She smiled, with her sweet face still close to his
own, for she had not risen as he had bidden her.

'Is it the old story, dad? After all this time—
nearly twelve months—is it possible that you are
thinking of Lord Thimberley? Well, if I grant
that I made a mistake, it is at least a mistake long
past mending. Let us dismiss that subject for ever.
Consider; he was two years older than my father!'

'If he had been two years older than your grandfather,' was his answer, as he shook himself free of
her embrace, 'the inducements would have been
the same. Of what consequence is the age of her
husband to a woman who respects herself? We
don't live nowadays in the Forest of Arden! A
girl like you'—he glanced at her sharply as she

stood a little turned away from him—'might have had society at her feet, and could have chosen her friends with discretion. It is not to be forgiven that you have had such a chance and turned your back on it.'

'I know, I know,' she cried eagerly, 'that the only way to your favour was to make myself unworthy of it! But why, I ask again, do you rake up these miserable ashes of our feud to-day? It can do no good—under any view of the case my repentance would come too late.'

A look of painful eagerness came into Mr. Denison's face; he put his hand in the pocket of his loose gown, and pulled out a letter.

'Read that,' he said, 'and let me hear reason from you at last.'

The letter was from her friend and chaperon, Mrs. Anstruther, and was addressed to Mr. Denison as a privileged communication. She told him that she had met Lord Thimberley a few days previously, and that he had anxiously sounded her in respect

to Margery, giving her to understand that if the
young lady was still free he was as bound as ever.
'He seemed delighted,' the letter ran, 'at the turn
of affairs with young Gilbert Yorke—I mean, that
he succeeds to the property only on the condition
that he marries his cousin. Lord Thimberley
looked upon him, whether with or without reason,
as his most dangerous rival. A word of encouragement would bring his lordship to The Chace.'

It is embarrassing when reading a letter to know
that your face is being closely watched in order
to discover the effect produced. Margery's grew
crimson under Mr. Denison's gaze.

'Is this true?' she asked, nerving herself to look
up boldly. 'I had not heard of it before.'

'It is scarcely likely that you should. A man of
Lord Thimberley's age and position would think
twice before he exposed himself a second time to
the insult of rejection.'

'I did not mean that. I mean is it true that Sir
Owen Yorke has made such a will?'

A muttered expletive passed Mr. Denison's lips. It was very seldom that he was betrayed into an oath; a weakness, indeed, to which men of a different temperament—less acid and close-textured than his own—are more prone. But the present provocaticn he found too much for him.

'Am I to believe,' he demanded, in a voice shaken with passion, exacerbated by pain, 'am I to believe that Lord Thimberley's suspicion is correct, and that it is this half-bred, fiddling jackanapes that stands between you and him? By——'

But before the word could escape him, Margery had interrupted him with an almost passionate disclaimer.

'No, no; it is not true. On my honour, it is not true!'

He made a movement as if he would have drawn her towards him, but stopped short, lest endearment should be premature.

'Do not trifle with me!' he urged. 'I cannot

bear it! I am suffering the torments of the damned. Speak the one word I want!'

His drawn, white face tore the girl's heart with pity.

'Oh, let me help you to the couch!' she entreated, trying to put her strong young arms about him and raise him from his chair, but he pushed her away with a violent effort.

'Answer, or leave me,' he said, in gasps of speech; 'and if you answer amiss, I care not if I never see your face again. You have thwarted me from the hour of your birth!'

'Ah, yes,' she returned, with half-playful but generous indulgence, 'I know what a cruel disappointment that must have been; but, consider, that was not my fault, and ever since I have been trying to make up for it——'

He interrupted her angrily, rocking himself at the same time backwards and forwards in his chair.

'Words, mere words! The power to do is in

your own hands again. In what sense am I to answer the letter ? Speak, or go !'

It was a crisis in her life, balanced, as it were, by a thread. Had there been a touch of tender-ness in his appeal—the least response to her sym-pathy—the chances are she would have yielded. As it was, the expression of the eyes gazing into her own hardened her heart. Was she to sacrifice her life, with all its untasked energies of love and happiness, to the selfish ambition of a father, who regarded her very existence as a superfluity, and who could derive from the sacrifice no real personal benefit ?

At the same time she dared not openly defy him : not that she lacked courage, but because his suffer-ings were so severe.

'I cannot decide on the spot,' she said at length ; 'you must give me a little time to consider ;' and then she added, with a tone and gesture hard to resist : 'But must I go away ? Will you not let me try and help you a little ? Williams is out this afternoon ; but I am as good as he, if you will only believe it.'

Williams was Mr. Denison's valet and nurse, and in the paroxysms of his master's neuralgic malady often brought him relief by friction and certain modes of manipulation in advance of the massage of to-day.

Almost to Margery's surprise her father yielded, and suffered her to help him to the sofa. In truth, his pain was overmastering, and there was something in the girl's abundant health and vigour that excited in his morbid and envenomed mind the desire to put its resources to the proof. Added to this, sympathy so eager and outspoken as hers always produced a sense of humiliation in his mind.

'Come,' he said with a sneer, as she knelt on the floor beside him, and prepared to fulfil her task, 'come and let us see how long your precious pity will sustain you !'

Margery was no saint, and the tone and implication brought the fire to the eyes that were so tender a moment before. Some impulsive protest rushed to her lips, but she checked it. The physical distress of the man before her would alone have braced her to heroic patience, even if he had not been her father.

As it was, she added to her protracted service the sacrifice of silence.

# CHAPTER V.

THERE are moods of mind when it seems as if the convictions and beliefs of a lifetime were overthrown, and the faculty of readjustment lost.

When Margery Denison was at length released by her father from attendance, she went to her own room, and locked the door with the feeling that no privacy could be deep enough.

The sick man's provocations had been, if not beyond the endurance of her strained self-control, at least beyond the power of her forgiveness. The relations between father and daughter had always been unhappy to the point of being unnatural; his cold-blooded selfishness was so absolute that filial feeling was an impossibility.

Her own training had been, as we know, defective and haphazard. She had grown up without being brought into intimate contact with anyone worthy of respect or imitation; and all that there was of good and noble in her was the spontaneous outcome of a fine nature, quickened into fruitfulness by reflection and imagination.

It seems a curious fact to record, but the girl had never seen an example of unselfish devotion until circumstances made her acquainted with Christina Yorke and her son. It was a spiritual revelation, and taught her a lesson she never forgot, developing in her ardent young mind the ambition to be magnanimous—an ambition that slackened inevitably under the severe tests to which her home-life exposed it.

The two years she spent in Paris under Mme. Coligny's care had done her good; the whole environment was pleasant and wholesome, and the teaching she received renewed her moral aspiration, and saved her from drifting into aimlessness and indifference.

But at the period of her return to The Chace her father had taken up his permanent abode there, renouncing the occasional absences which had helped to make life bearable.

Then had followed her London campaign. She was perfectly aware with what object her father and her aunt strained their meagre resources to provide the expenses of these seasons in town, and, in a qualified sense, she was prepared to forward it. Against a purely mercenary marriage her will was indignantly set, but there was just the possibility that fortune might be so singularly kind as to bring to her feet some suitor who possessed the qualifications insisted upon by her father, as well as those which made up her own ideal.

Do not conclude that this ideal was extravagant. We desire, for the most part, what we miss, and the virtue that ranked supreme in Margery Denison's mind, and which she thought would suffice to win her reverence and love, was the virtue of unselfishness — a quality of shy growth in the heated atmosphere of London society.

Since the failure of his hopes—now, unhappily, resuscitated—Mr. Denison had reluctantly abandoned the idea of mending his broken fortunes at his daughter's expense : he had made great sacrifices, and they had been rendered abortive, not by the stubbornness of circumstance, but by her own —a course of conduct which deserved to be visited with harsher penalties than a sick man had the power to inflict.

He succeeded fairly well, however, in making the proud, solitary, sensitive girl acutely miserable, in spite of the natural high flow of her spirits and energy. Well for her that the old Broadwood still stood in the library, and that she had the power of losing the sense of personal pain in the pages of a book, in the glory of a sunset, or in noble sympathy with the sufferings of her thankless persecutor.

But on this Sunday in question, after she was set at liberty by Mr. Denison, the power of mental resilience seemed to have deserted her. True, she was now free—this matchless Midsummer evening —to go where she liked and do what she liked, as her father had told her, but when does fate seem more ironical than in providing the opportunity without the means of improving it? What could she do? Where could she go?

She and her aunt had long been cut off even from such society as the neighbourhood offered, for Mr. Denison's pride was of the kind which made him feel all courtesy and hospitality that could not be repaid to the uttermost farthing, as an offence and a burden. He had given his daughter her chances, which she had flung ignominiously away; henceforth he was justified in constraining her to submit to the social seclusion that suited himself, and Margery was too proud to complain.

But to-day, as she sat wearily on the deep-cushioned seat beneath her windows, with her arms crossed on the sill, and her aching head bowed upon them, the desire for companionship and sympathy burned hot within her.

She thought of Gilbert Yorke, and dismissed his idea with a tender smile; did no other obstacle stand between them, the strong objection manifested by Sir Owen Yorke to their intimacy would have sufficed, for her pride was as tenacious as the sense of poverty alone can render it.

Then she asked herself a question which she had never asked herself before—namely, whether to marry Lord Thimberley was not perhaps, after all, the best thing she could do? He was a well-intentioned, honourable man, one who had proved himself faithful and disinterested beyond most, and he would make life—life that was becoming day by day more insupportable—very easy for her.

She decided to consider the argument out of doors—but before going out she would drink a cup of tea with her aunt, and tell her that she felt that she stood in need of a walk. It was never Margery's habit to draw upon Mrs. Sutherland's sympathy; her brother gave his sister her own burden to bear, and hers was the nature that solicits support but is never competent to yield it.

Half an hour later saw Margery walking swiftly down the avenue of limes towards the gates that led out upon the public highroad, though at this point it was a very secluded one. Her feeling was to put a long distance between herself and her unhappy home, and to breathe some purer air than that which shut it in. She walked swiftly, though her limbs were still cramped and tired and the evening was hot, because she was of that eager temper which makes the body obedient to the motions of the mind, and hers was in a state of strong excitement.

It is one of the dicta of the exemplary Southey that there are few troubles that cannot be *walked down;* but Margery had walked some miles before she was conscious of much improvement in her condition.

Then she drew rein, as it were, and looked about her to try and ascertain where she was, heaving at the same time a heavy sigh, partly from the fatigue of which she had not been conscious in her deep brooding thought, and partly to dismiss the weight of the controversy which oppressed her.

She perceived that she had reached a neighbouring village, which lay beyond the limits of her usual walks, but which she distinctly remembered having been taken to by her nurse as a child.

Leaning against a gate which opened on a pasture-field where some cattle were grazing, Margery paused and gazed.

The scene before her was not particularly picturesque, but there was a homely charm about it that pleased her in her present mood better than beauty. The sun was still more than a full hour above the horizon, its slanting beams falling on cottage roofs and gardens that seemed eloquent of Sunday quiet. Were their inhabitants all abroad, and if so, where? She saw no groups of idlers sauntering in the fields, or dotting the long lane that stretched to her right.

Possibly, she thought, with an indulgent smile, they were all assembled within the walls of the humble slated, red-brick meeting-house which filled the foreground of her picture, and which is a familiar object in most of the villages of the West Riding.

The country was but scantily wooded, but close to the spot where Margery stood a tall sycamore-tree was planted, and as she looked up it was into a delicious mass of pale pendent blossoms, clustering under the fresh leafage, while higher still the swallow and the swift were careering, with wings sharply pencilled against the deep-blue sky. From the wayside hedges came the sweet smell of the wild-rose and the honeysuckle, and in the remote distance the gray-green moors rose in undulating masses, cutting the sky-line.

Margery gazed until she felt her eyes were full of tears; the silence and the peace seemed to deepen the weight at her heart, and to aggravate her troubles. The very keenness of her relish for all the innocent pleasures of life seemed to mock the incongruity of the cramped and maimed existence she was condemned to lead.

It was all so intolerable that she had been driven to face an alternative more intolerable still.

At this moment a harsh sound broke the silence, and called off Margery's attention from herself. She perceived that it was the opening of the chapel door, which squeaked on its hinges, and that a woman came out carrying a crying baby in her arms. Margery watched her with a sympathetic smile as she made her way to one of the more distant cottages.

'Poor soul,' she said to herself; 'she will take it hard that she has lost the sermon!'

The chapel-door remained open—indeed, that it should ever have been shut in such weather upon the crowded congregation was marvellous—and Margery heard that a hymn was being raised.

The voices of the singers were not highly trained, according to the canons of Italian opera; but the gift of fine natural organs and of musical perception is part and parcel of a Yorkshireman's inheritance, and the girl listened with a sort of gracious allowance that quickened into a sense of pain and yearning.

Unable to distinguish the words at the distance, and yet drawn by a curious spiritual magnetism, she approached the building closer, and, looking in, her presence was at once detected; and a man sitting near the door arose and invited her to enter.

Margery obeyed and placed herself in a quiet corner, anxious to escape as much as possible from the observation she had already aroused. Indeed, the man's accost had been so friendly, and she was so weary both in body and mind, that the proposal was a grateful one. Nor was the scene altogether unfamiliar to her, for in her neglected childhood she had often accompanied the few servants of the house to their respective chapels, and they had been, if larger, almost on the same lines as the bare, clean, barrack - like room in which she now found herself.

She was quite aware that this was one of the Wesleyan village chapels sown broadcast over the country by the zeal of the Connexion, and served, for the most part, by young men on their probation.

The pews were of white deal, straight and narrow, in order to economize space, and destitute of any provision for the weakness of the flesh; and at the further end was the pulpit, a round wooden box raised considerably above the ground. Margery wondered whether the preachers who occupied it, and who gazed around from this coign of 'vantage, had any adequate perception of the crude ugliness of their surroundings, and, if so, whether it damped or stimulated their ardour.

The chapel was quite full, in spite of the witching beauty of the world outside; for the most part the audience seemed to be country folk, but there was a considerable scattering of people evidently of a higher grade, and an alert and expectant air was easy to be detected in the aspect of all.

'Some favourite preacher is doubtless expected,' thought Margery, with a touch of cynical amusement, promising herself half an hour's distraction in criticising the oratorical results of imperfect culture and experience of life, combined with self-confidence and effusive pietism.

The hymn, which she discovered was the one before the sermon, was now finished, and the congregation settled firmly in their places. There had been an energetic use of pocket-handkerchiefs, performed with an unmistakable air of finality, as well as a clearing of the throat, which, it may be observed, is often a sympathetic sound in a public assembly.

Margery began to wonder where the minister could have hidden himself, seeing no concealment seemed possible within the four corners of the chapel, or whether he had not yet arrived, when the problem was solved—almost to the upsetting

of her gravity—by his suddenly rising, and dis-
closing himself from within the deep-seated shelter
of the pulpit.

It was obvious he could not be a tall man. He
stood for a moment or two in silence and surveyed
his audience, not with the underbred, official confidence for which Margery was prepared, but with
a large, luminous gaze that conveyed the idea both
of penetration and of benignity. She had an uneasy conviction that his eyes, which were very fine
eyes, had rested for a moment upon her, knowing
that her white gown and broad-brimmed hat made
her conspicuous.

He chose for his text the words spoken by St.
Paul in his speech before Agrippa: 'I was not
disobedient unto the heavenly vision.'

He had probably read and expounded the chapter
earlier in the service, as he seemed to credit his
congregation with a knowledge of the circumstances.

Perhaps there are few things more unsatisfactory

than the summary of a sermon, simply because the effect produced depends so much upon the individuality of the speaker and the quality of his voice. But there is scarcely any form of speech more influential when gifts of heart and brain are united to favourable physical conditions.

All these things seemed present to Margery's judgment in the sermon to which she was called upon to listen. In the first place, the young minister possessed that quality of sincerity and naturalness which captures the heart; and nature had been kind enough to endow him with a voice at once clear and sonorous, yet capable of the most delicate modulations.

The leading idea was that in the experience of every human being that of St. Paul was repeated— that to each man and woman, according to their respective sphere and individuality, the Divine challenge came, and that the issues of life depended on the measure of obedience paid to it. He sketched rapidly, but, it seemed to her, with the hand of a scholar and a master, the conditions which made up the experience and moulded the character of Saul of Tarsus, and the completeness of his self-renunciation. To this height of sacrifice few were called, but the obligation was binding upon every soul.

'The true reward of life,' he said, 'for which alone its race should be run, is the inner life nobly lived, not the outer one richly recompensed.'

And then he went into homely detail, showing such intimate knowledge of the trials and sorrows of humble lives, and with the temptations which so desperately beset them, that the eager upturned faces of the men and women listening to him softened and glowed under his words, and ejaculations of conviction and of religious aspiration broke from the lips of many.

Long before the conclusion of the sermon Margery had rightly established the identity of the preacher. He was John Cartwright, Martin Cartwright's son, and the bosom friend of Gilbert Yorke, now passed out of the age of hobbledehoyism, under which she remembered him, and become an accredited minister of his Church.

But what development of heart and brain had taken place since then! His words had sent a wave of spiritual aspiration across her own soul, and endowed the conditions of her daily life with new possibilities, amongst which scarcely seemed that of marrying Lord Thimberley.

She rose and left the chapel before the conclusion of the service, slowly retracing her homeward way under a sunset sky of pearl and rose and amber— fit ending to a perfect day. She walked slowly, partly because she was subdued and thoughtful, partly in the hope that John Cartwright, whose way, she thought, must lie the same as hers, would overtake her.

He did so by the time that she had passed through the village, and had reached the comparative seclusion of the dull turnpike road, which stretched between it and The Chace.

On hearing footsteps behind her, easily discrimi-
nated, for they were rapid and firm, unlike the
heavy tread of the rustic, Margery turned round
and spoke to him.

' May I shake hands with you, Mr. Cartwright ?'
she said, smiling, and holding out her hand with a
delightful mixture of friendliness and interest, and
with the unconventional frankness that was one of
her greatest charms. 'You did me a great service
many years ago, and I have never been able to
thank you for it.'

And then she added, looking half shyly into the
magnificent dark eyes that were fixed on her face :

' I think you have done me another this evening.'

John Cartwright out of the pulpit was a different
man from what he was in it. He blushed violently
under the young lady's words, and seemed at a
loss for a reply, finally murmuring indistinctly
something to the effect ' that he had no recol-
lection of ever having been able to serve Miss
Denison.'

The embarrassment of a man whom you know to be able is a subtle compliment no woman is likely to mistake, and Margery found herself better pleased with her companion than she had expected.

'I will recall the circumstance,' she said sweetly, 'since our road lies in the same direction. But let me explain to you why I am alone. I came out for a walk this afternoon, with no intention of going so far; then I looked into your chapel and was entrapped, first by the kindness of your people, and then by your eloquence, Mr. Cartwright.'

John smiled, this time with quiet self-possession.

'I am not an eloquent man, Miss Denison. If you were able to listen to me with patience, I expect it was because there was something in what I said that fell in with your mood of mind. That makes us very tolerant of imperfection.'

'We will put it in that way if you like it best,

and there is some truth in it. You see, if one is living a very meagre, not to say sordid life, one is glad to catch at anything that can throw a gleam across it. I can read your face, Mr. Cartwright: you are saying to yourself that, of course, I am speaking from the point of view of other people— that a girl who lives in a big house and goes up to London for the season can know nothing of that kind of thing from her own experience. But you are mistaken !'

' If,' he answered, ' I was inclined to doubt whether the expressions " meagre and sordid " could be rightly used as applying to, Miss Denison's life, it was not because of the reasons she mentions.'

' At least,' said Margery, ' you may take my word for it that there was not a poor woman listening to you this evening who stood more in need of help and consolation than I. Your anti-dotes commend themselves to my imagination, and, with some of us, that is a great help to practice.

You see, it would make things easier if, instead of kicking against the pricks, I could regard them as so many divine messengers between God and my soul. It would give an unction to the difficulties and troubles of my daily life to persuade myself that, by patient endurance of them, I was graduating for the palm of the saint or the crown of the martyr. Religion, after all, is only a compromise—a sort of spiritual diplomacy.'

'Yes,' he said quietly, 'that form of religion has been recognised from the beginning, and judgment pronounced against it—"Whosoever will save his life shall lose it." The religion that lives is not self-regarding, and finds its motive power elsewhere than in the contingent crown and palm.'

She looked at him steadily. 'And what is that motive power?' she asked.

'I think it has as many modifications as there are recipients; but the root of the matter is always the same—love to God and to man; not self-love under any of its disguises.'

'You discourage your neophytes, Mr. Cartwright. Some of us are so made that we must make our own miserable egotism a stepping-stone to higher things. I tell you frankly that I have been applying your sermon to my own case. I am in a very great difficulty! There is a worldly way of extrication, and I suppose there is a better one. The question, which cannot be decided otherwise than on personal grounds, is, which shall I choose?'

The manner was gay and animated, but there was an undertone of recklessness and bitterness which was fully detected by her companion. He had, in common with the rest of the neighbourhood, some knowledge of the state of matters at The Chace, and a much more intimate comprehension from what Gilbert Yorke had told him. He even leaped to the conclusion that Margery's last words pointed to the alternative of a marriage of interest, the contingency which overshadowed his cousin's life. If so, his duty as a friend and as a teacher were at one.

'I suppose,' he said, 'some such temptation as that you speak of besets us at all times, but it narrows itself to a very simple point, the choice between good and evil. To decide that it is hardly necessary to take divine motives into account, for lower ones will serve—the ultimate disappointment we inflict on ourselves by wrong-doing as well as the misery upon others.

'We are all so linked together,' he went on, his swarthy cheek flushing with a sense of guilty consciousness, 'that we never do wrong only at our own cost—this one and the other suffer with us.'

Margery smiled. 'You are very wise for so young a man, and one—pardon me—whose experience cannot be very wide. But shall we walk a little faster? I want to reach home as soon as possible. They will be anxious about me, and with some people, you know, anxiety always takes the form of anger. I feel almost as much a culprit to-night as I did years ago, when I stole out of the house to meet poor Gilbert Yorke in the Iddersleigh meadows. Ah, that reminds me! The service I have never thanked you for was the delivery of my message to him. Take my thanks now, please.'

John smiled a little wistfully.

'Poor Gilbert! I hope the adventure did not cost you, Miss Denison, as much as it cost him;' and then, as she looked inquiry, he related the circumstances of that memorable evening in a way admirably calculated to kindle her admiration for the loyalty of her boyish lover.

'I wonder your conscience allowed you to give him my message,' she remarked.

'It did not. I transgressed my conscience.'

'Have you repented and made atonement?' she asked, her face lighting up with humour.

'I have repented,' he replied very gravely; 'it is not often put into our power to make atonement.'

She made a quick movement of deprecation, but did not speak; she was examining her own conscience.

For a little time they walked on in silence. Then she asked :

'Have you heard from your cousin lately?'

'Do you not know he is ill?' John exclaimed in surprise. 'He is down with fever at Vienna, or he would have been present at Sir Owen Yorke's funeral. If I can get leave of absence, I am going to him to-morrow.'

Margery stood still; the news was so sudden it seemed to take away her breath.

'You do not mean his life is in danger?' she demanded.

'No, no, it is a mild case, and he is well nursed; only he has expressed a wish to see me—not, be assured, from any apprehension of death, but from the natural desire to have an old friend near him. You may perhaps find it hard to believe,' he added, with his illuminating smile, 'but Gilbert and I are as good friends as when we were boys together. No more faithful heart ever beat.'

'I have no difficulty at all in believing that you make a good friend, Mr. Cartwright.'

'If you mean that you find it easier to believe this of me than of my cousin, Miss Denison, you make a mistake. I am not more trustworthy because I am dour and unattractive — it is the clearness of mountain - pools that masks their depth.'

Margery smiled, looking at the speaker with an expression both arch and kindly. His sincerity was evident, and his humility touched her.

John felt uneasy under that lingering regard, conscious of sensations that he regarded as shameful. It was as if a spark of fire shot through him from heart to brain, making his face flush and his pulses tingle.

They were now close upon the gates of The Chace, and Margery stopped and once more held out her hand.

'Thank you, do not come any farther. I suppose you are going to walk into Copplestone.

I hope your mother is well? I always presume
to admire Mrs. Cartwright so much. I think she
has such a noble face.'

' She is a noble woman,' was his answer.

It struck Margery that he spoke without enthusiasm ; but, then, she was apt to gauge a son's
attitude towards his mother by the feeling that
had bound Gilbert Yorke to the dying Christina.
John had raised his hat, and was pursuing his
way, when Margery called him back.

' If you should go to Vienna,' she said, hesitating
and blushing a little, not from any self-conscious-
ness so much as because John's penetrating eyes
were fixed on her face, ' will you send us news of
your cousin ? My aunt is very fond of him, and
he and I have been good comrades for more years
than I shall soon care to remember.'

' Certainly I will write to Mrs. Sutherland—as
Gilbert's amanuensis.'

' Will you stay long ?' she pursued. ' Because, if
not, do not take the trouble to write. It will not

be worth while. Come and see us at The Chace when you come back, and give us a *vivâ-voce* report, which is so much more satisfactory.'

She read refusal on his lips, and anticipated it by a little trick of coquetry, which entirely imposed on his simplicity.

'We shall both be so deeply anxious for news of Gilbert,' she said softly—'such news as only an eye-witness can give.'

'Then I will come.' And this time he turned away with an air of resolution that made Margery smile as she walked slowly towards the house.

# CHAPTER VI.

MARGERY entered the house by the open library windows, seeing at a glance that there was no one but Mrs. Sutherland in the room.

The lady was seated in a deep-cushioned chair, with a book between her fingers; but it was too dusk to read—the evening too lovely for lights—and she was dozing gently.

Margery's entrance aroused her. She sat up with sudden alertness, as if prepared to challenge any imputation of slumber; and, in order to maintain her position, she spoke with unusual asperity.

' At last! Where, in Heaven's name, have you

been? Do you know you have been gone for hours? Your father has led me a pretty life!'

Margery glanced at the book in her hand. It was not light enough to read the title, but the familiar label of the circulating library could be easily distinguished.

'Ah!' she said, putting off her hat and sinking on the cushion at her aunt's feet, 'I see your book has been stupid! Forgive me, dear; I did not mean to stay out so long—I will tell you all about it presently. But, first, has dad been tormenting you about Lord Thimberley?'

'My dear, there is no more to be said on the subject—such fidelity ought to be rewarded; and now that poor Gilbert Yorke's chances are gone, you have no inducement to refuse. I am sorry. I never liked any young man so well as poor Gilbert; but, as I say, all that is over. It seems providential—I mean, that this should have happened before it was too late.'

'What should have happened?'

'Old Sir Owen's death and his extraordinary will. Why, he has always snubbed that girl shamefully, and now to force the young fellow into marrying her! It is too bad. Had he been free to choose where he loved, I would not have said a word against it, in spite of the title, though it is hard for any woman to turn her back on a coronet. But, as things have turned out, Madge, you must reward the Viscount.'

'Have you said this to my father?'

'I told him I would use what influence I had, but that I did not think there would be much difficulty in the matter. Of course, dear, now that poor Gilbert Yorke is put out of court—you know what my feelings have always been on this matter——'

Margery made an impatient gesture. 'Spare me "poor Gilbert Yorke"!' she cried passionately. 'Have I not told you again and again he was nothing to me but a friend? I would not have married him, except out of kindness, perhaps, if he

had come to me free, with the title-deeds of Rookhurst in his hand.'

Mrs. Sutherland drew a breath of relief.

' Yes, dear, I know you have told me so before,
but I never believed you until now. Is it pride,
Madge, because that spiteful old man has arranged
things so cruelly ? I should be grieved, dear.'

' No, auntie, it is the law of contradiction. We
never love the men who adore us, and whom we
loved when we were little girls. I am very fond of
Gilbert, very, very sorry for him, but I do not want
to marry him, and I never did.'

' Dear me, what a comfort !' said Mrs. Sutherland briskly. ' You have quite cheered me up, and
I had got very low, sitting alone so long after being
so grossly insulted by my poor brother. But,
there, we will say no more about that ! Brighter
days are in store for us. Poor Lord Thimberley,
how delighted he will be ! I never knew of a man
more in earnest. You will let your father write to
him to-morrow ?'

Margery rose slowly, and took up her hat, as if to leave the room; then stood, looking out into the glimmering twilight. A voice was in her ears that seemed to have a singular power of influence, 'We never do wrong at our own cost alone.' She recalled with the exactness of a delicate musical ear the precise inflection of the speaker, 'This one and the other suffer with us.'

She turned round to Mrs. Sutherland.

'Auntie,' she said, 'I have forgotten my bad news. I happened to meet the Rev. John Cartwright, "poor Gilbert's" cousin, you know, and he told me that he was ill of fever at Vienna—so ill that he is going to nurse him.'

The desired diversion was made. Mrs. Sutherland was full of instant concern, and closely examined Margery as to her knowledge of particulars.

'You know my views,' she observed; 'there never was a more charming young fellow than poor Gilbert Yorke! It would be a dreadful pity if he were to be cut off just at the moment he comes into his inheritance, in spite of the hard conditions attached to it. My poor darling,' laying a kind hand on the tall, white-robed figure; 'I am afraid you will be feeling it dreadfully!'

'I am,' said Margery, in a low tone, and turning away her face, that glowed with a secret shame. 'I am! Dear auntie, you will make it plain to my father that I must not be pressed to any decision while my old friend lies between life and death. If he heard of my engagement——' She stopped short.

Mrs. Sutherland sighed. In a moment Margery's arms were round her neck, and her kiss on her faded cheek.

'No, no,' she cried, 'I will tell him myself! It was a cowardly baseness to ask you to do it.'

Her aunt sighed again, and pressed the girl closer.

'My dear,' she said, 'I think it will be better

to leave it to me; he can't say quite as hard things to me as to you, or at least not the same. After all your denials, Madge, I don't seem quite sure you know your own mind, but at any rate it would be hard, I allow, to send for Lord Thimberley at such a crisis as this. So we will agree to wait a few days and see how things turn out. I have no doubt he will get better; still, if he were to die, though of course it would be very dreadful, it would get over a good many difficulties on his side, as well as ours. It stands to reason he must hate that girl.'

Margery's cheek had blanched.

'If he were to die!' But no, that eager, many-sided vitality had surely too strong a grip on life, and was not to be snuffed out like a spent candle. 'Oh!' she said, with a forced laugh, 'he is not going to die.'

'No, my dear, of course not; so ring for lights and the supper-tray. How I do hate our early dinner on Sunday! Then you shall sing to me,

" Oh, rest in the Lord!" or anything else you like. You know my views—I always sleep better after a little sacred music when one is not able to go to church.'

# CHAPTER VII.

## OLD AND NEW LIGHTS.

'You have made up your mind, John—you refuse to wait till after the quarterly meeting?'

It was Mrs. Cartwright who spoke, sitting in her accustomed chair in the dining-room of Elm Grove, and addressing her son almost in the same tone of authority as she had used years ago.

The aspect of the room, however, was a little unfamiliar, for the weather was so warm that no fire burned in the grate, although it was duly laid for lighting. Mrs. Cartwright never allowed any frippery of summer decoration to insult the instincts of North-Country comfort. Her own chair, too, had been placed near the window, which was set open, giving a pleasant view of the well-kept grass-plot sloping towards the public road, and of the trim flower-beds.

John, who looked as if he had just come in from a walk, and had walked far, was standing opposite his mother, hat in hand, leaning against the window-frame. He did not answer immediately, and she spoke again.

'You know our hopes—your father's and mine—that you may be recommended and nominated next March to our own circuit, and that we may hear your voice in Castle Street Chapel. Many things are in your favour, but there have been some breaches of discipline, as when you absented yourself two years ago from the same mistaken sense of duty as now, and it will tell against you seriously if your place is found empty again. I do not think the necessary explanation will help your interests much, namely, that you are gone to the gayest capital in Europe to visit a friend outside your own social sphere, who is known as one of the most worldly and dissolute members of a society where all are seekers after pleasure and deniers of God.'

John smiled, a grave, quiet smile that provoked the old Adam in his mother's breast.

'I am going,' he said, 'to visit a sick man who wants me sorely on matters of pressing importance, and who is not dissolute—pardon me, mother—if I am compelled to grant that he is worldly.'

He was going on, but Mrs. Cartwright interrupted him.

' What took you, then, to Monte Carlo two years ago? John, you cut me to the heart!—your moral sense is warped by this insane weakness. I always foresaw it would be like this!'

He would have approached to soothe her, but she motioned him away.

' After all these years of watchfulness and prayer,' she said, in the sharp, cutting tone of suppressed anguish, ' you will make shipwreck of your faith, and become a beacon and a byword !

Who knows what the travail of my soul has been for you? and it will have been in vain. Where can I blame myself? Perhaps much might have been better done, but I have striven to do my best, and the shortness of human foresight who can help?'

Then she added, with intense bitterness:

'You are a teacher of men; tell me what a mother ought to do when she sees a child exposed to desperate peril and has no power to save him. Does her responsibility cease? But I waste words!'

Her dark eyes seemed to emit sparks of fire as she looked at him.

In the attitude of John Cartwright's mind towards his mother there was doubtless a certain hardness which, while he deplored and condemned, he seemed unable to overcome. Perhaps, too, in this relation he lacked perception. The intense mother-love, though held in the leash of her iron will, had been discerned by young Gilbert Yorke, and had almost drawn his own heart towards her; but then his perceptions were quickened by the most tender of personal experiences.

But John had no such aids to comprehension. The repression of his childhood and youth had left its indelible traces on mind and character. He could not know that the hand that chastened, or the voice that condemned, were the instruments of a passionate love that bled with secret anguish at the necessity; for the mother kept the counsel of her heart too well.

It is a rare case when a child, suffering from the effects of discipline, comprehends or accepts the motives; but the fault is not with the child. As John grew older, intellect as well as feeling revolted from the austerity of his training; he felt that in shutting out pleasure from his life, as though pleasure in itself were sin, his moral nature had been dwarfed and stunted.

Then had occurred the brief episode of his cousin's coming amongst them, and the consequent rebound of his imprisoned faculties. The spell of Gilbert's individuality conquered both heart and mind. For the first time he seemed able to warm himself at the fires of life. The ardour of the one thawed the ice of the other; the ready speech unlocked the silent tongue; the efficient sweetness soothed and satisfied the aching yearning of a life-time—a lifetime of seventeen years !

It seemed to John Cartwright as if the smile of God had been consciously shed upon his path, and that his mother had stepped in and darkened it again. Matured intelligence, with an ever-deepening sense of the needs of others, had served to help him to appreciate both the integrity of her motives and to wear off the sharp edges of his bereavement; but even now, as he stood listening to her passionate protest, indignation rather than sympathy was the feeling excited.

' I waste words !' she repeated, in a voice that now shook as much with anger as with sorrow.

'You are right,' was John's answer; and his face warmed with a light that she knew to her cost only one subject could kindle, 'words are wasted when they are used to defame my cousin Gilbert, and shake my feeling for him. Even if he were all that you think him, or worse, my duty would be plain—to cleave to him in the hope of saving him. But it is not so. Without any profession of goodness he has always set me lessons in patience and self-denial that I should find it hard to follow, and, with every temptation to go wrong, he manages to escape evil by force of some indwelling faculty that I do not think it profane to believe may be the Spirit of God. We know not whence it comes or whither it goeth,' he quoted, with his illuminating smile. 'Bear with me, mother.'

'And was it this indwelling Spirit that led him to the tables at Monte Carlo? May God forgive the blasphemy!'

'You are again under a mistaken impression.

What we heard was grossly exaggerated; and I feared, as you feared, that he was exactly of the temper to fall under the power of this vice. But —I have told you all this before—he had really staked very little, and at first more from the pressure put upon him by others than from any craving of his own. I do not deny that he was bitten by the poison, and under its horrible fascination; but, that being the case, so much the greater was the sacrifice that he never hesitated to make. For Gilbert to turn his back upon the most delirious of the devil's delights, in order to pacify the conscience of a friend, was not likely to reduce that friend's love for him.'

Mrs. Cartwright made a movement of intolerable impatience.

' We will waive all further discussion. There is only one point I care to carry. Go, if you will, since you are too old to be coerced, and my influence is as nothing; but return again in time for the quarterly meeting on Friday.'

John deliberated. The day was Monday, and the interval was so brief that it would hardly allow of Gilbert's rallying from the excitement of meeting before the pain of separation was forced upon him; on the other hand, filial obedience had been the rule of his life, and was accepted by him as an absolute duty.

His mother spoke again.

'Do you suppose,' she asked, 'that the reputed heir of Sir Owen Yorke and the favourite subordinate of a great man—for so you tell me he is—will not be well housed and well nursed? There will be no physical needs to supply, and, taking your estimate, he is already a vessel of grace. Therefore, the only object of your visit is the personal gratification of indulging that misplaced affection which lies at the root of your neglect of natural duty. Three days may suffice for this self-indulgence.'

John looked up with a flash of indignation, but he expressed it after his own fashion.

'Mother, I wonder if we shall ever understand each other? You said just now I was too old to be coerced; that is, I suppose, in the old fashion; but there is not much gained so long as you keep the power of applying the lash where you know me to be most sensitive. It shall be as you wish. Unless it should be a case of life or death, I will be home by Friday.'

John started for town by the afternoon express from Copplestone, and pursued his journey without rest or pause. He arrived at Vienna on the evening of a day when a great social function was in progress at the English Embassy.

It had never come in his way before to get a glimpse of such magnificence as he now saw around him, while he was being conducted to the upper chamber occupied by his friend. As he passed through halls and corridors, where half-opened doors revealed interiors that dazzled his eyes, he received a new and extraordinary impression of all that might be included in the phrase, 'the pride of life.'

The crowd of servants he encountered, the delicious odours that seemed at once to soothe and stimulate, and came he knew not whence, the beauty of the women who had passed him on stair or landing in such superb apparel that he thought it must have outblazed the typical glory of Solomon, and a nameless air of distinction in the men, appealed to faculties never before called into exercise.

At one point he passed the open door of the ball-room, and involuntarily he stood still. It was empty of guests for the time, for dancing was not yet, but it was flooded with the soft radiance of wax candles, and the light was thrown upon walls draped at intervals with Oriental tissues, and all the spaces between, from frieze to dado, filled in with roses, contrasted and harmonized through all the tints of their exquisite variety. At the upper end, amidst a grove of palms and lilies, cunningly concealing the musicians' gallery, a slender fountain threw up its tube of perfumed water almost to the height of the roof, scattering its sparkling dew around.

It was a glimpse into an unknown world, a world where the desire of the eye assumed such enchanting proportions that it was transformed and glorified. The wealth lavished upon those odorous walls, which the morning's sunshine would blast, staggered the imagination of the young Methodist minister.

Another hour, perhaps, and the room would be filled with the men and the women he had seen, and music, exquisitely performed, would add the crowning element of seduction to one of the most potent of the world's delights.

What, after all, did he, or his mother, or any member of the Connexion at Copplestone, know of the force of worldly temptation ? Such a world as he now faintly guessed at was outside not only their experience, but their conception. It had been outside his.

And yet there were men, names fragrant in their
country's memory, both dead and living, who kept
their conscience clear and did their daily duty,
with this voice of Circe at their ears. Again, the
sick man he was going to see—his cousin, Gilbert
Yorke—was, he supposed, an item in this overwhelming account, admitted by right of birth into
the innermost circle of the social elect, his natural
gifts and graces being so much over and above.
And yet how unspoiled he was! Just as simple
and natural and kind to himself, when he had
come a year ago to see them all at Elm Lodge,
as on the first memorable day of their meeting.

John's heart swelled as he recalled his mother's
words.

At length the room occupied by Gilbert Yorke
was reached, and the man who had accompanied
John knocked at the door. In a moment it was
opened by a woman clad in the garments of a con-
ventual nurse, who closed it again behind her, and
stood confronting them in the passage.

A few words in rapid German, exchanged with his guide, which exceeded John's comprehension of the language, and the sight of his own card, put her in possession of the situation. She turned to him with a smile of engaging kindness, and a baffling interrogation in an unknown tongue. With inward sinking of heart John replied to her in French, explaining that, badly as he spoke the language, he spoke German still worse.

She answered, also in French, and assured him, with an air of perfect sincerity, that he spoke the language to perfection ; that his friend was greatly better, was expecting him 'avec toute impatience,' but that it was too late to see him that night ; nor was she to be moved by John's fallen countenance, or his gallant attempts to convey entreaty and expostulation through the halting medium of a foreign tongue.

She dismissed him with permission to call the next morning, ' but not before twelve o'clock.'

John was sorely disappointed, but he was also

dead tired. He found a hotel, supped, and went
to bed, but was awake so early the following morning that there remained hours at his command
before it would be time to keep his appointment.
After breakfast he wandered somewhat vaguely
about the city, and whiled away a portion of his
tedious leisure in pursuing the interminable circuit
of the magnificent boulevard, the Ring Strasse,
and trying to interest himself in the impressive
antiquities of the Innere Stadt. Then he diverged
towards the heart's-core of the capital, threading
the narrow and irregular streets with a sort of
suspended interest, gazing now at the lofty tower
of the Cathedral of St. Stephen, with an instinctive perception of the incongruity—however skil-
fully disguised—between the thirteenth and the
nineteenth centuries; and standing before the
Hofburg with the growing sense that in this
curious and composite structure, bearing on its
face the record of a thousand imperial years,
the idea of the divine right of kings might well

take root and flourish, planted on such prescrip-
tion.

He was too preoccupied for interiors—nor, perhaps, did he know the priceless treasures which
this interior contained. He found his way to the
spacious, cheery quay of Franz Joseph, paced for
some distance along the canal, retraced his steps,
and at length saw that there was barely enough
time left to find his devious way back to the Land-
strasse before noon. The clock struck twelve as he
mounted the stairs of the Embassy, and a few
minutes later found him face to face with his
cousin.

Gilbert was dressed in a loose gown, and was
lying back on the cushions of an invalid-chair,
with a little table at his elbow, and a closed porce-
lain stove in the middle of the room. To John's
eyes, albeit not unaccustomed to sickness, his
aspect was so reduced and wan that it needed an
effort to check an exclamation of dismay.

But the keen bright eyes of the Sister he had

seen the day before, who now sat sewing near the
window, were upon him, and he could not fail to
understand the gesture with which she touched her
lip with her finger.

'M. Yorke a l'air tout-à-fait ravissant aujourd'hui,'
she said, rising and approaching her patient, who
had held out a weak hand to his friend, and tried
to speak, but some weakness choked his voice.

John sat down near him, and began to talk of
his journey, and the impression the great capital
had made on his mind, in such a cool, quiet fashion
that he won golden opinions from Sister Félicie,
who presently returned to her seat by the window,
but not before she had administered a cupful of
what looked like very weak broth to the invalid.

Then Gilbert said, with a smile that brought
back more of the old look to his face:

'Next to my mother, Jack—would you believe I
have fretted for her like a child?—I am glad
to see you. It is the kindest thing you ever
did.'

These words satisfied John. Since last night a doubt had found its way into his mind whether, through an intimate association with a different class in society, Gilbert might not have forgotten how rough he himself was, how redolent of Yorkshire soil. Therefore the expression of full contentment with which his cousin, as he lay back in his chair, looked him over from head to foot was doubly welcome, and quickened the sense of gratitude that formed so strong an element of his friendship. No doubt he betrayed the softness of his feelings in the tender consideration with which he answered and anticipated Gilbert's questions, for the latter said, in his old manner:

'I think you have grown in grace, Jack! You couldn't possibly be better than you were, but you are sweeter. I suppose, too, you are in full orders now—how proud your mother must be of you! Some of us get all we want.' He sighed.

The other did not sigh, because it was not his

way to give feeling so easy a vent, but the careless words smote him with a pang.

Then, very soon afterwards, to John's indignant surprise, Sister Félicie stepped forward to cut short the interview and dismiss him, and this before a word had been spoken on the subject uppermost in the minds of both — the kindred themes of Margery Denison and Sir Owen's will.

The strength of his feeling left him speechless, but Gilbert begged for a little further indulgence.

'We will not talk, dear Sister, but let him sit here an hour longer. I grow stronger by looking at him. I smell the breath of the moors.'

'Que voulez vous?' she answered, shaking her head, and addressing John with her fingers on Gilbert's wrist. 'Je ne puis rien y faire! Allons, demain viendra!' And with this poor encouragement John was constrained to take his reluctant leave.

This was not the recompense for which he had

undertaken a long journey; his notion had been to
have planted himself by his cousin's bed or chair,
and to spend all the hours of the day, not to say
the night, in close attendance.

He passed the rest of the day in a religious
observance of the duties of a flying tourist, and
he wrote to his mother; but his heart was not in
his work, and he counted the hours lost till he
again found himself admitted to Gilbert's room.

Sister Félicie was full of conversation; she had
to tell him how fortunate it was that he had not
stayed longer yesterday, as, soon after he was gone,
his Excellency himself had called in 'to see *mon-
sieur*, and the doctors in consultation had congratulated her that her patient had borne the strain
so well.

'They placed me in good hands,' said Gilbert,
looking at her gratefully. 'In typhoid, Jack, it is
not the doctor, but the nurse, who saves.'

She looked inquiry, and he repeated in German
what he had said, with an added touch of kindliness.

Sister Félicie blushed and smiled, and, perhaps in virtue of the recognition, consented on this occasion to leave the young men alone together, explaining that she would be within call in the adjoining room.

With a sigh of satisfaction John drew his chair close to Gilbert's, the little table standing between them, on which had been placed a bundle of letters and a cup of the same decoction he had seen administered yesterday.

'You look better to-day,' he said wistfully, and laying his hand on the feeble fingers that were idly pulling at the tape that bound the letters together; 'but are you sure, old fellow, that they give you enough to eat?'

'They tell me so, and my faith is implicit; strong meat is not for babes, and you will soon see, I'm afraid, that there's not much manhood left in me.'

His lips twitched a little, and the eyes that looked into John's had a suspicious brightness.

John cast his own steadily on the floor, and set his lips firm.

'How long can you stay, Jack?' continued Gilbert. 'A week? a fortnight? I am hardly fit for this business to-day'—he touched the letters again.

Perhaps in the whole course of his life John Cartwright had never known a feeling of sharper pain or more bitter resentment. The promise extorted from him by his mother would make of this his farewell visit. He was at a loss how to answer, but Gilbert came to his relief.

'I see—I was unreasonable. Of course, you have your own work to do.' Then, looking again into his friend's face, he asked, almost with a cry, 'Jack, must you go to-day?'

'Yes,' returned the other, with a sort of stricken doggedness. 'I have promised—I must go home to-day.'

Then silence fell between them. Gilbert lay back with closed eyes, looking very white and still,

and John sat and watched him.   Presently he said
in an altered voice :

'My promise was not unconditional.   I shall
*not* go to-day.   Drink a drop of this stuff, Gilbert.'

Gilbert roused and obeyed with a faint smile.

'Give me a few minutes' grace.   I told you how
it would be.   Typhoid, Jack, more than anything
else, I believe, makes one realize your mother's
dictum that " we are but dust and ashes." '

John rose up sharply.

'Let us put these papers away,' he said.   'Is
there a place into which I can throw them ?   We
will have nothing to say to them to-day.   I shall
be here the same time to-morrow.   Indeed, for that
matter, I shall stay over Sunday.'

Gilbert put out his hand to restrain the action.

'That won't do now.   I shall never rest again
till I know the truth.   You must humour me,
Jack.   Opposition will be worse than indulgence.'
He paused, then went on : 'My poor grandfather !
I got the news of his illness and death in the same

day. It was at the beginning of my illness. The doctors would not let me move, and since then I have been worse, and know nothing.'

'Nothing!' repeated John apprehensively.

'Ah, then the news is bad! I was afraid of it, and had not pluck enough to open these letters, though they were given me half an hour before you came in. You know what I am afraid of—not for my own sake, but for hers, which means for the sake of her people—that he has cheated my hopes.'

'I know. I quite understand.'

Gilbert's face flushed and quickened.

'It would be a lie to say I did not wish him to disinherit my cousin Edward. I did wish it, and have leaned upon hints and promises. You will understand, Jack, that the poor fellow has no power to spend or enjoy more than he has got— nor half so much—and that I——'

He stopped.

'Gilbert,' said John sternly, 'I will not hear

another word.  I shall call your nurse—I will go—
if you like, to return later.'

He was crossing the room, but his cousin's weak
voice had power to stop him.

' That would be cruel kindness, Jack.  I should
have a relapse, for certain.  I wanted to defend
myself from being a cad, but let that go.  You
know it all as well as I do—I have loved her since
I was sixteen—I have not a hope outside of her.
For her sweet sake I have kept my life pure as her
own, and—for that same sweet sake I wish to
supplant my cousin.'

John looked straight before him, holding his
peace.  Gilbert seized his hand, if so feeble a grip
may deserve the word.

' You know something, I see—the local gossip !
Tell me, Jack ; I can bear it better from you.'

John Cartwright's integrity had never been put
to a more severe test.  The sight of the thin
flushed face, the eagerness of the eyes, in which
foreboding already seemed to touch despair, cut

him to the quick. He was also terribly afraid of
the consequences of this agitation, and yet hesitation would be almost as dangerous as the truth.

It was not possible for him to tell a lie (though
he almost wished it were), but to temporize was
imperative.

'Of course,' he said as quietly as his leaping
pulses would let him—'of course some rumours
have reached us, but they are so contradictory we
do not know what to believe. One thing,' he
added, feeling himself to be a traitor as he spoke,
'is generally accepted as true—that Mr. Edward
Yorke is not your grandfather's heir.'

'You know more—for God's sake do not kill me
with this cruel kindness!'

'I do not know more. In telling you this, I tell
you more than I know.'

Gilbert looked at him steadily, but the other bore
the investigation without flinching.

'Then we will both inform ourselves. Mr. Percival's letter is here. Read it to me, Jack.'

John opened his lips to protest, but he saw all protest was vain.

'If you refuse to read it, I shall read it for myself, and my head is scarcely equal to that. I see there is something wrong. It may be bad for me to know the truth, but it is better than suspense. Don't be afraid. I shall bear it like a man.'

There seemed no alternative. Gilbert pulled himself together, sipped his meagre restorative, and encouraged the other with a smile.

'I imagine the worst is always past when the victim has settled his head on the block,' he said.

John broke the seal of the lawyer's letter, and began to read.

After a few formal condolences on Gilbert's illness, and the information that Sir Owen Yorke's will had been made public immediately after the funeral, according to the testator's instructions, Mr. Percival took the trouble to enumerate the names of the guests present at the double ceremony, amongst them being those of Mrs. Yorke and her

daughter. He then gave a summary of the afore-
said will, laying great stress on the extent and value
of the inheritance to which Gilbert succeeded—the
estates of Rookhurst, Yorkshire, and of Holywells,
Norfolk; the stocks and shares soundly invested ;
the plate, pictures, and furniture of the respective
mansions; everything, in fact, by which it was in
the power of his late client to mark his affection
for his grandson, on the sole condition that he
should marry his cousin, Philippa Yorke, within a
year of the testator's decease.

The effort which it cost John Cartwright to pro-
nounce these last words was only to be equalled by
the desperate courage with which Gilbert Yorke
braced himself to hear them.

'Thank you, old fellow,' he said, as John dropped
the paper, and raised his eyes slowly to look at the
effect of his work ; 'it is not so bad as I feared.
We shall get over that!'

John still gazed at him, but was not deceived.
The rush of his feelings—of indignation and ruth,

of love and closest sympathy—was so violent as to break down his judgment, and prompt him to do a very foolish thing. True, he hesitated a few moments, while prudence whispered in his ear, and during this brief interval he moved away from the table and stood by the window, which looked down, as from an eyry, on the courtyard of the house.

Carriages were dashing in and out, crowds of people coming and going, all eagerly intent on the pleasure or business of life, and this upper chamber where the common tragedy of blighted hopes was being enacted seemed curiously aloof from it all.

Why should he hold back the drop of consolation that might assuage the anguish of his friend?

He spoke without turning round.

'I think and hope that is not impossible,' he said, answering Gilbert's last words. 'A man like me has, of course, little knowledge of these things; but I saw Miss Denison last Sunday—I will tell you all about it presently—and I cannot help thinking that—that she cares for you. In that case, wealth is not everything; you will be able to persuade her.'

'Ah, don't torment me, Jack! Tell me all at once.'

And John, still keeping his post at the window, told him his tale. He had the genius of a Boswell, and not a word or gesture of his subject went unchronicled. The lambent flame of his own passion played round all Margery's manifestations, and glorified them; but the use he made of it was to show her more clearly to his friend, and to strengthen his failing heart by, deductions religiously believed in by himself.

Gilbert hung upon his words, his sanguine nature embracing the possibilities almost as assurance. He had covered his face with his hands to hide its workings.

'Bless you, Jack!' he said, after a long pause had fallen between them, 'you have given me new life. I shall get strong by leaps and bounds. If she really cares for me—but I dare not dwell on

the thought.   It has always been the dream of my
life to work for her.   I would ask for nothing better
than to earn our living—say, in the orchestra here
—and pour the weekly wages in her lap.   Ah, how
happy we might be!'

'I don't think that would do,' said John grimly.

'Did I not say it was a dream?   I am not such
a fool as to expect a girl like her to accept such a
position.   But I have good prospects of advance-
ment otherwise, and, if it were necessary, I would
even never speak to my fiddle again, but turn what
wits I have to the one object of wriggling myself
higher in the service.   Sir Hugh Dalrymple is
very kind to me.'

John looked at him.

'I don't know how any woman could resist you.'

'Ah, but that is your mistake.   I am not the
sort that women go mad about, or give up all for.
I always feel myself a poor thing, with no depths
to sound, nor any of those twists and reserves of
character   which   provoke   curiosity—wearing   my

heart on my sleeve. For that matter, Jack, you are far more interesting than I. I can fancy if you were in society——'

'But I am not,' interrupted his cousin sharply, and at the same moment Sister Félicie entered the room with her watch in her hand and her finger pointing to the dial.

John rose immediately to take his leave. 'Till to-morrow,' he said, holding Gilbert's hand, but Gilbert shook his head.

'I will see you no more till we meet at Rookhurst. Do you wish your mother to hate me worse than she does? No, Jack, you have done me all the good you can. I should not sleep to-night if I did not know that you were steaming away to home and duty. I shall follow sooner than you think.'

# CHAPTER VIII.

## 'OH, WRETCHED MAN THAT I AM!'

THE conditions of Sir Owen's will threw Mrs. Yorke into a state of mental and moral confusion.

The will was an act of atrocious injustice in the interests of a young man whom she ardently disliked on the most legitimate grounds for a mother; but there was an equivalent, doubtless, in the possibility that the wrong done to the son might be redressed to the daughter. The crucial question was, would it be thus redressed? Of her daughter's interest in the new heir she had not a doubt; it had been one of her many provocations, and, indeed, she had sometimes been disposed to attribute the increasing listlessness of Philippa's manner, and the low tone of her health, to a secret pining after her cousin, who had always contrived to make himself as agreeable to the sister as odious to the brother, on the few occasions when they had met. That Gilbert did not return Philippa's unconscious devotion Mrs. Yorke felt perfectly sure, but feeling was of small account in the balance of a splendid inheritance. Still, one point was to be allowed for—the young man was distinctly crotchety.

There was no minute discussion of the terms of the grandfather's will until after their return home from Rookhurst. The disinherited heir, as both himself and his mother considered him to be, had been discreetly forewarned by letter, so that the first fury of his disappointment might be spent; but if such had been the case, the portion still left was a very ugly and formidable residuum. He insisted upon the presence of his sister, who had wished to excuse herself, before he would 'open his mind,' as he called it, on the subject.

'Look here, old lady,' he said, addressing his mother in the offensive phraseology he sometimes adopted, 'you wouldn't mind, would you, spending your precious legacy in trying to upset this confounded will? How was it the young thief wasn't there himself?'

Philippa sat in the background out of the range of the speaker's sight; there was something in this combination of malignity and physical helplessness that always made her feel cold and frightened.

Mrs. Yorke, who herself had a half-terror of her unhappy son, explained that Gilbert Yorke was ill at Vienna of typhoid fever.

'Typhoid!' cried Edward, almost with a shriek; 'people die of typhoid most times, don't they—though I guess no such luck will be ours. Would to God I could stand by his bedside and give him his next dose! I always hated him; I hate him now like—hell!'

Philippa rose from her chair, white and trembling, but resolute.

'I won't stay in the room to hear such language,' she said; 'it is horrible! He has always been good to you. Mother, why do you allow it?'

'Oh, ho!' sneered her brother, 'is that the game?—on his side instead of ours, grabbing at the fortune that belongs to me, and shall never be either yours nor his if I can hinder. Cripple as I am, it shall go hard if I don't spoil your little game, miss!'

'Edward,' said his mother sternly, 'you forget yourself! A gentleman should try and behave with decency, even under such a provocation as yours. Your sister has had no hand in this miserable business, and if you were generous you would be glad there is a chance of her getting what you lose.'

The young man stretched himself on his couch, and flung his arms above his head with an ostentatious yawn. This violence of temper always came in spurts, but the mood it left behind was hardly to be preferred.

'Don't preach,' he said; 'it's too late in the day.  Gilbert Yorke gets my fortune if he marries Phil—therefore he doesn't marry her!  Unless he would rather let go the fortune than take her, in which case it might suit my book to help Phil.'

He looked towards her with a malicious grin.

'Mother!' cried the girl appealingly.

'My dear,' replied Mrs. Yorke soothingly, for she was touched, and almost alarmed, at the look of anguish on Philippa's face, 'is it worth while to take any notice of what Ted says when he is out of temper?  There is every excuse for him this time.  Run out into the garden, child, and forget all about it.'

Philippa was prompt to obey, and it must be owned that her mother did not linger long behind her.

'I will send Fletcher to you, dear,' she said to her son as she retreated.

He gnashed his teeth as the door closed upon

her, half in rage, but it must be owned half in pain and sorrow too.

'What a helpless log I am!' was the thought of his mind. 'Others can get away from me, but, hang it, I can't get away from myself! I should like to cut and run after that girl, and tease her till she cries, wretched little traitor as she is! But she has the whip hand of me!'

And then, for his faculties were at full stretch with excitement, the notion took possession of him that things would have been very different if he had been, as he ought, Sir Owen's heir. Now he was nothing but his mother's dependent, and might be slighted with impunity; then, with riches and influence at command, his word would have been law to his household.

Amongst the better feelings of his nature was a sort of dog-like attachment to the family seat of Rookhurst. When staying there as a guest, as had happened frequently during the last few years, and stretched on his couch in the pleasant oriel room over the gateway, he had dreamed one of his few dreams. He had planned the alterations he would make, and even advanced so far as designing a sort of invalid carriage in which he might be able to go over the estate with his steward to survey the farms.

And now all that was over. Another would reign there in his stead, leaving him only the mockery of an empty title, and that other was the possessor in double measure of every good gift that had been denied himself. Therefore he was justified in detesting him.

'Always good to me,' he said to himself, repeating his sister's words; 'so much the worse for his impudence! He knew that he had got the length of the old fool's foot, and could afford to be civil. It drives me mad to think that he will be able to take his full fling in the world while I lie rotting here. What else is left me but to plot and plan how best I can serve him out—with or without Phil?'

The man was malignant and contemptible, but he was profoundly to be pitied. Unhappily the inability to enjoy does not destroy the desire for enjoyment, and there were times, as now, when the phantasmagoria of the world's delights passed before his eyes and mocked his helplessness, till he could have shrieked aloud with pain and rage.

He that is without sin amongst us, let him cast the first stone.

# CHAPTER IX.

## JOHN CARTWRIGHT GOES TO THE CHACE.

THE day following John Cartwright's return from
Vienna the quarterly meeting, which was regarded
as so important a transaction, was duly held.

There was much that was trying to flesh and
blood in the ordeal, all the more because an almost
morbid shyness—seldom shaken off, except in the
pulpit, or where some equally powerful influence
was at work—as well as an acute sensibility, were
hidden under the awkwardness and reserve of his
usual manner. Added to this, he knew the extreme
anxiety of his mother as to the issue, believing (but
in this he did her an injustice) that she would
gauge his intellectual and spiritual position accord-

ing to the judgment of the influential members of the Connexion.

The decision, however, was favourable to Mrs. Cartwright's hopes. The testimony borne to her son's scholarship, his devotion to duty as shown in his work amongst the poor and in the schools, and his acceptance as local preacher, was so unanimous that permission was given, according to the known wishes of the honoured superintendent of Castle Street Chapel, and other influential members of the district, that John Cartwright should be appointed as assistant-minister and be allowed the privilege, as the only child of his parents, of continuing to live under his father's roof.

Some of the ministers who came from a distance, and a few personal friends, were invited to dine after the meeting at the house of Martin Cartwright, whose efficient hospitality had a wide reputation.

When John came downstairs, a few minutes before the arrival of the guests, he found that his mother was giving some last touches to the dinner-table, and he followed her into the room.

The table was glittering with fine glass and silver, and she was placing little bouquets of roses and ferns within the old-fashioned finger-glasses; decanters full of gold and crimson wine shed their glowing colours on the fine white damask. The garden window stood a little open, for the weather was very sultry, and the dinner-hour was six o'clock. It would be eaten in the full light of the summer day.

Her face softened and warmed as, looking up at the opening door, she recognised her son. John saw and understood, and, the look in her eyes encouraging him, he went up to her—a little tentatively, it must be owned—and kissed her.

'Mother,' he said, 'do you know how beautiful you are?'

She smiled and blushed a little. 'I believe I was once,' she answered; 'and I am glad my son thinks me so still, because I know he sets so great a store by beauty. It is a snare, John.'

The words chilled him. He seldom contested a point with his mother, which was perhaps a mistake; but the force of habit is well-nigh irresistible, and repression had been the habit of his life. It had been in his mind to tell her all about his recent visit, and how things which were the talk of the neighbourhood really affected Gilbert, but the inclination had faded away.

Presently his genial father bustled in to take stock of the reserve of wine, in his character as butler of the establishment, and his face brightened as his eyes fell on mother and son.

'Eh, luve,' he said tenderly; 'but this is a proud day for both of us! Thy heart must have burned within thee at all the fine things said of John; and he deserved them, too, every word of them! Bless the lad, he has never cost us an hour's sorrow in his life!'

Instinctively John's eyes sought his mother's, and met hers fixed upon him with a look of such

passionate yearning that he was startled by its
intensity.

'My heart did burn within me,' she said softly;
'but I think, Martin, that the happiness of to-day
has been helped forward by some sad and anxious
hours. We never buy our blessedness cheap, but
win by what we lose.'

There was a knock at the door, and Mrs. Cartwright moved forward to receive her friends, leaving her son with an ache at his heart. He had
understood his mother to mean that he had gained
spiritually from what he felt to have been the
abiding loss of his life—the breaking off of household intercourse with his cousin. He resented the
implication with all the strength of his ardent feeling for Gilbert, and none the less strongly because
the fire of his generous indignation only burned
inwardly. He had ceased to try and show Gilbert
to his mother as he was, or as he thought he was.

Perhaps it was because of the discomfort caused
by this sense of the injustice done to Gilbert Yorke

that John Cartwright betook himself the next day to The Chace, and asked for Mrs. Sutherland.

The servant, who was scarcely so neat and deft as one of his mother's handmaidens, seemed at a loss for an answer, looking, John thought, not only perplexed but troubled, so that he felt it incumbent upon him to take himself away. It was possible, in spite of Margery's graciousness, that the lady might not care to count him amongst the people she received ; she was probably of the same temper as her brother, whose pride and exclusiveness, which always mounted higher in proportion to the descent of his fortunes, were a matter of public repute.

He had just put his card into the maid's hand, and was turning to the door, when he heard footsteps running down the broad shallow staircase, and Margery's voice in his ears.

' Please stop, Mr. Cartwright,' she said ; ' there has been some mistake : we want to see you very much.'

She dismissed the girl with a nod, opened the door of the library, which gave upon the hall, and motioned John to follow her. It was not till they were both within the room, and she had closed the door, that she turned fully round to him and held out her hand.

'Welcome home,' she said, 'from the finest capital in Europe! How abject must Copplestone appear in your eyes! And how did you leave—Gilbert Yorke?'

She spoke with a vivacity so forced that John, who had not till then had the opportunity of seeing her face, looked up in surprise.

She was standing before him in a gown of dark heliotrope silk that fell in straight folds from throat to feet, and flowed on the floor behind. To our young Methodist preacher it seemed a robe of splendour, though the wearer herself would probably have characterized it as 'an old tea-gown'; but it harmonized well with the tints of her complexion and the fine colouring of her eyes and hair.

A bunch of yellow roses, from the same tree as those he had last seen her wear, was fastened below the lace at her throat, and seemed to enclose her in a delicate perfume. John, who was himself conscious of a secret loss of self-control, having gazed for one brief moment, dropped his eyes, and Margery saw—for she was observing him closely, not to say defiantly—that the colour came into his face. The vision was dazzling, and he shrank sensitively from the full blast of the recognised temptation ; but there was more than that: Miss Denison's beautiful eyes were red with crying.

'Ah !' said Margery, raising her head and drawing up the figure which slightly overtopped John's, with an air in which pride and pathos and a sort of impatient scorn of herself were all mingled ; 'I see—you detect my weakness ! It is quite true—I have been crying like a child or a fool, too feeble to bear the brunt of my own purpose, and—I owe my present trouble to you.'

'To me !'

The tone expressed surprise and incredulity so sharply that Margery laughed, but John could perceive that the laughter was perilously near to tears. Perhaps she feared his penetration, for she turned away and began to walk slowly up and down the long room. She had taken up a large black fan from a table and fanned herself as she walked, the loose sleeve of her gown falling back and showing the beauty of her arm and the exquisite turn of the wrist. John's eyes followed her with fascinated intentness. His mother was right when she accused him of being too prone to the worship of beauty; he would have been its slave had not duty long had the upper hand of instinct. But the present was a strong temptation.

Beauty such as Margery Denison possessed had been held as paramount in circles where beautiful women were almost as plentiful as primroses in spring; to this shy and solitary observer, who had unconsciously enshrined her girlish loveliness in his heart as his ideal of what was adorable in the sex, her beauty, such as it now appeared, produced a depth of fine sensation that would have made the man of the world laugh, and perhaps would scarcely have been understood even by Gilbert Yorke himself.

'Yes,' she said at last, breaking the silence, and speaking slowly and softly, with half-closed eyes as if to concentrate her attention, or possibly from weariness; 'I am in trouble to-day more even than usual, for trouble is my daily portion, and I repeat, Mr. Cartwright, that I owe it to you.'

'Will you be pleased to explain?' he asked.

She did not answer at once, continuing her slow rhythmical motion through the room, but when she had again reached the spot where he was standing, she paused before him and said:

'When I say that I owe my present trouble to you, Mr. Cartwright, I pay you a compliment that is always welcome to the professional teachers of men. The Sunday before last I heard you preach a very stimulating sermon to the toilers and

moilers amidst the worries of life; but it had less
effect upon me than certain words spoken by you
on our homeward way. You see, I am talking to
you quite freely, as if we were friends of old
standing, and perhaps that strikes you as strange;
but I know you better than you think. I am quick
to understand people, and sermons—honest sermons, I mean—are always a revelation; and then
again, everyone who knows your cousin knows
you.'

She stopped, as if to give him the opportunity of
reply, but he was in no hurry to avail himself of
it. Perhaps few things could have distressed him
more than to be made the subject of her own
conversation, for he had all the morbid modesty of
the man who conscientiously undervalues himself,
and it seemed to him an absolute waste of time
that, when he was on the tenterhooks of anxiety
on her own behalf, and had come simply to tell
her about his friend, she chose to talk about
himself.

'If,' he said, 'any words spoken to me have brought trouble upon you——' Then he broke off with the dark flush on his cheek and the glow in his eyes which marked his moods of suppressed feeling. 'Forgive me, Miss Denison; to put the idea into words serves to show its presumptuous absurdity, only, however your trouble is caused, can I be of any—the humblest—use?'

'Yes,' was her answer, 'if you are able to give me the strength which, so far as I know, no one human creature ever yet gave to another. I am one of those people, Mr. Cartwright, who can take a leap into the air sometimes, but have no power of patient continuance in well-doing. Worse, if I ever do right I am sure to be sorry for it afterwards, and to make everyone about me miserable on the strength of it. I think it would be better if I went my natural way and had more courage to go wrong.'

Her face lighted up with a smile of pathetic humour.

' I see you do not follow me—you look delightfully perplexed.'

' I am perplexed, but not because I do not follow you; for, if I may speak of myself, over and over again I have set my will in advance of my inclinations, and suffered, and no doubt made others suffer too, in trying to reconcile them——'

Again he stopped short, for her eyes dwelt upon his face with a smiling interest that disturbed as much as it surprised him. She was so absolutely at her ease that all her powers of observation were at her command, and effectually obscured his. He began to wish that he had never come, and he would have gone away now, but that he had not yet touched on the matter which brought him.

Margery, who had been standing hitherto, now sat down in a low chair and signified to her guest to take a seat also. Then she resumed speech in her clear, vibrating tones, without a touch of hesitation.

' When I went into Stone Edge Chapel that

evening I had almost made up my mind to a course of conduct that was neither true nor honourable, but which had a great many advantages to recommend it. Now I have remade it, greatly in consequence of some things you then said or suggested. My father—I only summoned courage to tell him just now—is bitterly disappointed, and my poor aunt so upset that she can receive no visitors. When I heard your name I could not resist speaking to you. I am like a child who has braced itself to the point of swallowing a nauseous draught—I want to be commended—I want to be encouraged —and—consoled.'

Her eyes sparkled with self-irony, but he could see the pain and struggle behind them.

'I think I am so happy as to be able to do that,' he said, with an eagerness that was great enough to overcome his embarrassment. And then, disregarding the gesture by which she tried to check his words, and which was attributed by him to a woman's sweet shame-facedness, he poured forth the

story of his recent visit to Gilbert Yorke, presenting
his friend with such happy and tender touches that,
in spite of herself, Margery's reluctance to listen
was overcome.

As John talked, his eyes from time to time rested
on his companion, and he seemed to grasp with
added force the idea of the perfect fitness which
subsisted between his brilliant friend and this
beautiful girl who sat opposite to him, swaying her
fan with a stately, measured motion, and with
reserves of love and tenderness in the animated
gaze fixed on his face.   Margery, too, in spite of his
careful reticence, could not fail to be aware of the
impression on his mind, and while her pride
prompted her to keep her own counsel with this
comparative stranger, her honesty warned her to
undeceive him, if only that he might help to
undeceive the other.

'I should be sorry to think,' she said very
gravely, 'that your cousin felt any serious reluctance
to conform to the terms of his grandfather's will.

Sir Edward Yorke has cause to complain of injustice; but he is so disagreeable, I believe, that very little sympathy will be felt for him. His sister, on the other hand, is sweet and good, and might well be the choice of any man, even if she did not bring Rookhurst and Holywells in her hand.'

' No doubt that is true—for any man who has the power of choice left.'

John spoke in the lowest and most deprecating of tones; his manner would have been thoroughly appropriate to any man pleading his own cause.

Margery was conscious of a sudden and vexatious embarrassment which made their proximity irksome. She rose from her chair and went to the window, standing in anxious debate with her pride and her conscience, and looking intently meanwhile at the chipped margin of the fish-pond and the blasted willow.

' You put me in a very awkward position,' she said at last, speaking with her back towards him.

'I cannot pretend to misunderstand your meaning —perhaps your object, Mr. Cartwright—and yet it is no subject for discussion with a third person.'

'I beseech you,' he interrupted, 'to put no constraint upon yourself. My only motive was to let you know that he was better, and—I don't understand where I find the courage to be so bold— that circumstances known to yourself, and to me as his brother and friend, make obedience to the conditions of his grandfather's will impossible.'

He rose and took up his hat.

'No, do not go until I have made you understand that what your friend wants—and you for his sake —he cannot have.'

She had spoken so far turned away from him as before, but now she suddenly changed her position and faced him.

'Who can tell him this more kindly than you?' she asked, looking at him steadfastly with head erect, and a certain wistfulness of expression that touched John with a deep sense of pathos. 'Persuade him of it, Mr. Cartwright, and spare me.'

'I cannot do that, Miss Denison, and no man worthy of the name would take his dismissal by proxy.'

'Do you blame me?' she asked. 'Am I to be supposed to have done a good action in refusing a rich man because I do not love him, and a base one in refusing a poor man on the same grounds? Is your conscience to be hoodwinked by friendship to that extent?'

'My cousin is not a poor man,' was John's answer. 'He has every quality for distinction in his profession, and a provision under Sir Owen's will. He is sure to succeed, if he may not be said to have done so already, and all that is as nothing in comparison with a heart and temper that few men can resist, and no woman surely.'

'Who made you,' asked Margery coldly, 'a judge and a divider between us? A man, especially a recluse and a cleric, has no more power of knowing what is acceptable to us in your own sex, than of dictating the fashion of our gowns. Gilbert Yorke is all that you say, and, indeed, I have loved him from the first time I saw him, when he was holding his mother's head on his shoulder, and stroking her cheek untiringly in one of her paroxysms of neuralgia. Even then, Mr. Cartwright, she was a lovely woman, and he the sweetest lad my eyes ever beheld, before or since.'

'He is just as kind and sweet now, and seems to pass through the temptations of the world like the Hebrew children through the fire—unharmed and unsmirched.'

John's eyes were very soft and tender. Margery's rested upon him for a moment, and then an ironical smile touched her lips.

'David can scarcely be so guileless as his Jonathan! Had you a particle of worldly cunning,

Mr. Cartwright, or some glimmering perception of a woman's perversity, you would know that a little hearty abuse of your friend would serve your purpose better.'

She held out her hand as if to dismiss him, adding, with a return of the vivacity and spirit which never long deserted her:

'I think I have mastered your views on the subject under discussion. I am to yield either to the pressure put upon me by my own friends or by yours, quite irrespective of my personal feelings; and in that case there can be no doubt that a father's wishes are the most sacred, and should carry the day.'

'No,' returned John simply, 'I do not think that. I would not wish even Gilbert to be happy—nor your father, nor any other man—at the expense of your own integrity.'

'Would it not have been kinder and more human to have said "at the expense of my happiness"?' she asked.

'With you,' he said, looking firmly into her face, 'the two are identical.'

She smiled and flushed a little.

'Come and see us again,' she said softly. 'My aunt will like to talk to you.'

# CHAPTER X.

GILBERT arrived at Rookhurst in the most delightful weather. It was July, but the season had been
late and the woods and pastures had scarcely
passed the point of perfection. The gardens of
his charming demesne were in full glow of bloom,
and the tinkle of the old Italian fountain fell with
a sense of cool pleasantness on the ear. The
servants, with whom the young man had always
been a favourite, received him with the usual
welcome, to which was added the deference due to
their new master. The housekeeper, who had been
his father's nurse, showed a natural solicitude about

his health; the best rooms had been prepared for his accommodation, as well as a dinner planned on the same lines of epicurean completeness as those to which the late baronet had educated his staff.

'A morsel of fish and a cutlet, with a glass or two of Chablis, is all I want, Dixon,' said Gilbert, with a touch of impatience as he gave back the *menu* to the old butler, who had presented it to him with the established formality; 'but never mind,' he added quickly, seeing the look of disappointment in the man's face, 'we will go through with it.'

It was like the Prince Charming of the fairy tales returning to his Palace of Delights after a series of adventures, with the serious difference that no reward awaited him and that he felt conscious of a dreadful hollowness in the spectacle, almost as if he himself were an impostor. Brought into the close contact of possession with all that could make life desirable and tempt an ambitious woman, a

new mood took possession of him—one of revolt
against what seemed the mockery of fate. Why
had his grandfather gone down to his grave
grasping in his dead hand that liberty of choice
which alone could have given value to his gifts?
Had he been able to go to The Chace to-morrow—
or, say, the next day, when his looks would less
betray the fatigue of his journey and the traces of
his recent illness — as the unconditional heir of
Rookhurst and of Holywells, and of all the long-
hoarded and well-known resources of his pre-
decessor, he would have had more courage to plead
his suit, knowing that it would have had the
support of her family and her friends; and what
bliss it would have been to enrich her!

And yet if she loved him—and it was his trembling belief that she did that gave such persistency
to his purpose—would not the fact of the cruel
exigency of his situation suffice to break down her
reserves and hesitations and win her at last to
consent to take her place beside him? In days

gone by how eagerly she had agreed with him that 'only this and that' were necessary for happiness, and he could offer her much more than 'this and that.'

Gilbert began seriously to reckon his resources: the £500 a year that he would take under his grandfather's will as the alternative of a splendid inheritance; the considerable sum of money lying at his bankers' which remained over and above from his too munificent allowance; and the rents and incomings from his term of possession, to which he supposed his right would be indubitable. In addition, his salary of attaché, and chances of diplomatic promotion—Sir Hugh Dalrymple having parted from him with the most encouraging assurances—and the gayest capital and choicest society in Europe as the scene of his wife's triumphs.

Before the day was over the young man's spirits had risen under one view of his position, to sink again before the long light waned under another. Later, he got his violin and poured out heart and

soul on its strings, now taking a movement of
Beethoven, then a few complex and troubled
phrases from Bach, or, again, a piercing *Miserere*
from some old monastic score. The purity of his
tone and the splendid bowing that was one of his
most delightful characteristics as a musician, made
the interpretation such as to be almost too much
for his own endurance; he felt as if joy and
anguish were going on at the same time—flashes
of peace and thankfulness relieving the sense of
passion, of hindrance and of vexation.

'I thank God,' he said, bowing his head re-
verently, as he at length put down his violin, ' for
one good gift that neither man nor woman can
take away.'

He shut up the costly instrument in its inlaid
case with more care perhaps but less tenderness
than he had felt for the little fiddle, the gift of his
kind *maestro*, which he had brought with him from
his poor home in Florence to his uncle Martin's
house.

He slept soundly, and awoke strengthened and refreshed to breathe the life-giving moorland air wafted into his perfumed gardens, and to find on his breakfast-table the following note from Margery Denison :

'DEAR GILBERT AND OLD FRIEND,

'We hear that you are expected home to-day ; and we know that you have been very ill, so that we are anxious, my aunt and I, to see for ourselves that you are better. Please ask us, one of these long summer days, to Rookhurst, and show us all the glory thereof. I have never been there as a guest, though years ago I visited it as one of the public, and my aunt remembers to have dined there on the coming of age of your father. Ask no one to meet us unless it should be your dearest friend.'

The note was signed ' Your affectionate friend,' and there was a postcript, ' Do not answer this in person.'

This letter troubled Gilbert. The instinct of the lover was chilled by the familiar kindness of the style, and he disliked the idea of doing the honours of a place that his guests would find enchanting, and yet which he was bound to forego.

He answered at once, fixing a day two days in advance, and giving instructions to his servants that the dinner was to be simple and unostentatious, with no suggestion of display in any of the arrangements.

Then his thoughts turned to John Cartwright. Was it possible that either Margery or her aunt would prefer the presence of his friend? He did not know they were on terms of intimacy, and, for his own part, he would on this occasion prefer to dispense with it. He felt that the circumstances of the day would inevitably lead up to some moment when he should be unable to resist putting his fortune to the touch, and that he would rather endure the result, whether good or bad, alone, without observation or sympathy.

But as Margery had implied a wish, he wrote to John, stating the circumstances, and asking him to join them and stop with him a few days.

' To have you all to myself at Rookhurst, Jack,

will make Rookhurst worth having, if only for a year. Good God, how bitter I feel!'

The next day's post brought a formal note of acceptance from Mrs. Sutherland, to whom he had addressed his invitation, and a letter from John declining to come.

'I preach my first sermon in Castle Street Chapel next Sunday,' he wrote, 'and I am full of solemn perturbations and concealed excitement. I think my mother feels the same, but we do not speak of it together. So, you see, I should be unfit for the company of fine ladies—for yours I am never unfit—and I would have come to you if you had been alone. Take me next week instead. I know nothing so much like an Arabian Night's tale as to be your guest at Rookhurst—never mind for how long! One day shall be to us as a thousand years.'

# CHAPTER XI.

## THE WORLD WELL LOST FOR LOVE.

IT was the hour before dinner, and the day so far had been pronounced by Mrs. Sutherland 'a perfect success.'

'One of those, my dear Gilbert, that poor Madge and I will mark with a white stone—we have not many of them now.'

'Poor Madge' was standing just within the issue of the open window which led out upon the central quadrangle ; her soft silk gown was of the tint of her favourite roses, and the radiance of her aspect—the nobleness of her port and the brilliancy of her smile—made her aunt's expression sound like satire.

' It is true, however,' she said, meeting Gilbert's smile; ' my poor aunt and I have a bad time of it just now, for she is made to suffer for my sins. The one excuse for my father is that he suffers so terribly that it would be almost a baseness to resent his conduct or judge him apart from his provocations.'

There was an inflection of pathos in her voice that touched Gilbert to the quick and brought his resolution to a point.

All day, for his guests had arrived early, they had been together, wandering about the grounds, peeping into pineries and hothouses of a temperature that forbade investigation, sauntering through some of the glades of the park till the luncheon bell recalled them to the house. The meal had been so light and elegant, and so well designed to meet the feminine taste, that Sir Owen himself, had he been in the flesh, could have found no fault with it. And, what was more to the purpose in the young host's opinion, Margery had said it was an ideal feast worthy of Olympus itself, and that she had never known before how much of the *gourmande* was latent in her nature.

After lunch they had driven out for an hour or two, finding the neighbourhood as charming as all the other surroundings of this fortunate youth, and since then, in the pretty room below the gateway, Margery had distributed afternoon tea, under the influence of which Mrs. Sutherland had returned her pathetic thanks.

'I quite understand,' said Gilbert, replying to Margery's last words, 'and I know from my own experience how brutally selfish sickness makes us, but dismiss all such thoughts to-day! Come into the garden as far as the old fountain, and let us leave Mrs. Sutherland to rest a little before dinner.'

He turned to that lady, his manner being a trifle hurried and nervous.

'May I tuck you up comfortably on this couch?' he asked.

'Thanks, but I could not be more comfortable than I am.' She looked from him anxiously towards her niece, as if she wished to convey a warning. 'Margery will be tired, too,' she said. 'Could you not both stay indoors, and—suppose you were to get your violin? That would be delightful!'

'Pardon me, it is hopelessly out of tune. We will not walk far; only to the edge of the fountain, where you will have us in full view. Come, Margery!'

He smiled and held out his hand. There was a little touch of authority mixed with the natural and acquired charm of his manner that would have been hard to resist. Margery had no desire to resist it; she put her hand frankly in his, and they stepped out on the lawn together.

When they reached the fountain they sat down on the broad, sun-warmed margin, and Margery unfurled the crimson parasol she had brought out with her; both were bareheaded, and both loved to sit in the sun.

A little breeze had sprung up, and lightly ruffled the sparkling pool in the basin, towards which she leaned and dipped her finger-tips in the water ; the fine elastic turf beneath their feet was the outcome of generations of culture, and the one or two geometric flower-beds, with which it was discreetly starred, presented an exquisite study in Turkey carpeting. The full-clad trees around swayed and whispered lightly in their topmost twigs, and the fragrance of a hundred roses was disengaged and hung upon the air. Before them stood the old house itself, matchlessly picturesque, and on either hand the park rose and fell in delicious undulations, but in such a fashion as to leave open vistas to the Derbyshire hills.

Margery looked around her from one point of vantage to another, and then she said in the lowest possible voice :

'I never saw anything more beautiful or so much to be desired ! The lines have fallen to you and your cousin Philippa in very pleasant places.'

It was a woman's ruse. She knew what impended, and with the impetuosity of her character was anxious to rush through with it, all the more because she was a little uncertain of her own strength. Whether it were the discipline of sickness or the discipline of a court, or the result of the energy of his purpose, Margery had never found Gilbert Yorke so delightful and acceptable to her as on this day.

He looked up as she spoke with a smile.

'Thank you. You have broken the ice, Margery, and I am grateful. Of course you could not fail to know that I should not let this day pass without——' He had begun firmly, but her eyes were upon him, full of sweetness and kindness, and his self-control broke down a little.

'You understand,' he resumed, trying again to be calm and quiet. 'No professions nor disclosures are wanted from me. I love you more than ever —more than aught else. Nothing is of worth without you, so it is no sacrifice to let it go. Come to me, Margery, and I will make you happier than any woman was before!'

'My dear, my dear!' was her answer, with tears in her voice as in her eyes, 'this is madness, mere Midsummer madness! Do you think so meanly of me as that I would ruin your life and break another woman's heart? We are both bound hard and fast.'

The evasion of the words brought with them an almost overwhelming rush of hope. He seized the hand that was lying on the warm marble close to his own and said, in the suffocating voice of suppressed passion :

'At last—you own—you love me, Margery! At last! At last!'

She drew away her hand, and redressed her position with a sharp movement.

'You forget that we are in the open air, within eye-shot of we know not whom. If I am to talk to you—and I want to talk to you—you must control yourself and listen to reason. How many times have I told you that I love you—I will not insult

you by saying like a brother, nor is it like that—
but as the dearest and sweetest of friends? Let it
rest so, Bertie!'

'Oh yes, I will be content with that! Become
my wife, Madge, and you shall love me as few
women have loved their husbands, because no
husband yet has so adored his wife.'

She smiled and shook her head.

'Suppose—I trust to you as a gentleman to hear
me quietly—suppose you induced me to listen to
you. We should both outrage right and reason to
a degree that would justly cut us off from sympathy.
Your grandfather had a splendid fortune to leave,
and opposing claims to satisfy. He thought he
was doing what was right when he made you his
heir, and appointed the sister of the man he
disinherited to share the inheritance with you.
She is young, she is sweet, she is good. If you
turn your back upon her you offer her a cruel
insult, aggravated by the greatness of what you
forego. As for me—hear me out, Gilbert—were I

inclined, which I am not, to listen to you, my poor father would curse me with bell and candle, and I should still further embitter, and perhaps hasten, the end which cannot be very far off. The punishment would fall on my aunt also, who has been good to me all my life. But even this is not the worst; I should hamper and impoverish the man who loves me, and to whom riches and all that riches bring are only a proper appendage, and in return for his mistaken devotion I should make his life thoroughly miserable.'

He had restrained himself with difficulty up to this point, but now he broke in impetuously.

'How could that be, when you had given me the desire of my heart? I am neither thankless nor inconstant. To have you so close that nothing could divide us would animate me to reach a point I should never touch otherwise, and inspire me with an invincible power to make you happy. No, let me speak, Margery, it is my turn! I am not a sentimental boy any longer, but have learnt what

women want, and would not begrudge your beauty
its privileges or its triumphs.  You should know
the great world and be known of it—all your
pleasures and successes should be mine.  I would
only bargain for little snatches of quiet—such as
we have had as boy and girl together when the
others were elsewhere, and I had my little fiddle in
my arms and you listened all eager delight, and
our hearts were so full that they could hold no
more.'

He stopped, and silence fell between them, filled
in by the plash and fall of the fountain.

Then Margery said : ' If I ask you a question,
do not be deceived by it, as if I were wavering
in my resolution.  Only tell me where the
means for carrying out your idyll are to come
from.'

He told her quietly and without exaggeration,
though all his pulses were leaping with the hope
she bade him relinquish.

Margery listened without interruption and with

the tender indulgent smile that had very little encouragement in it.

'My dear Gilbert,' she answered when he had done, looking at him with eyes in which kindness and mockery were at strife, 'it would take at least two-thirds of the income you speak of to supply me with gowns suitable for these Viennese functions. I have no generosity to match yours and should inevitably hate the man whom I had made poor. Give up your dream, my friend.' She cast a swift inclusive glance around and added :

'Nothing surely can be easier than to reconcile yourself to realities !'

She rose as she spoke, as if to intimate that the controversy was over, and as she stood for a moment on the lawn before him, she shook out the shimmering folds of her gown and raised her hands to arrange her slightly disordered hair with a little air of weariness, real or affected. Every movement was singularly graceful and alluring. Gilbert had not risen, but sat watching her.

'There is one question,' he said in a muffled voice, 'that I should like to ask you, if it did not seem like a baseness to ask it. Would you have answered me like this if I could have given you Rookhurst as well as—my soul and body?'

She flashed down upon him a glance of superb indignation.

'I refuse to answer! And yet—have I not given proof—there is no indelicacy in alluding to what all the world knows—that I am not one of the women willing to sell themselves?'

'Forgive me. I did not dare to imply that. What I want to know and cannot rest without knowing is simply this—my poverty, poverty that seems to me affluence, is the bar between us? *Otherwise*, Margery, *otherwise!*'

She turned and began to walk towards the house, so that he was obliged to rise and walk beside her.

'You have not answered me,' he said. 'Do you know that I think I could leave you better if you loved me!'

'A paradox,' she answered, 'that, if it admit of explanation at all, does so on lines of such utter selfishness that I will not admit your testimony against yourself. You mean'—with a sparkle of humour in her glance —'that you would sleep better to-night if you knew I was crying my eyes out for hopeless love of you?'

'Yes,' he said seriously; 'I acknowledge that I should.'

'And after such a confession you expect to retain my regard?'

'Ah, regard!' he rejoined eagerly; 'there it is! I am not satisfied with your "regard." I would have you regard me differently. If I thought you would go home to-day and weep for me, I should thank God and take courage, for then I should feel sure that, sooner or later, you would dare the shame of poverty for my sake.'

'I never said *shame*, Bertie, and you are quite mistaken. If I loved you with all my heart and soul—but I do, I do; I love you with both!—but if

I loved you passionately, inordinately—as a woman shouldn't—I think I should be able to keep my secret. I will not frustrate your grandfather nor rob you of your inheritance. You would soon regret it when struggling uphill with a penniless wife behind; nor, worst of all, will I shut the door upon your cousin's splendid prospects.'

' Under any circumstances I shall not marry my cousin.'

Margery looked curiously at his white, set face.

' That is, of course, for your own decision,' she said coldly. 'At least, I have announced mine. And now I am glad to see my aunt coming to meet us. We shall have nothing more to say to each other this evening than a friendly good-bye.'

# CHAPTER XII.

THE growth of a reputation is a very curious thing, the progress and results varying beyond all calculation.

One fact at this time was being recognised at Copplestone and far beyond its boundaries (for the ramifications of the Connexion spread far and wide), namely, that John Cartwright was becoming a power in his Church.

As a preacher his influence grew slowly but surely; he was quite deficient in the fluent, melodious flow and splendid wordiness on which so many men build up their claim to a following. From the depths of a mind that had dwelt long and exhaustively on the principles and doctrines of Christianity, and that had itself endured the unspeakable anguish of doubt and religious eclipse, he reasoned and convinced on the grounds of his thorough equipment, of his deep personal convictions—now founded like a tower of strength, impregnable to sway or shock—and of the wide humanity of his nature. Without impassioned appeals or rush of language, he seemed able to lay his hand on the springs of conscience and feeling, and to make the belief that animated or exercised his own soul vibrate responsively in those of his hearers.

When this sort of spiritual magnetism exists it has a reflex power, for the audience which has been strongly moved by the thought of the speaker sends back the wave of sensation to his own heart and brain with accumulated energy.

But character exercises a still greater influence than utterance ; and in John Cartwright there was a singleness, a directness and a strength of daily purpose that seemed always equal and always trustworthy. To make, according to his opportunity, the world better than he found it, and if possible happier, summed up the objects of his life; nor did he wait for great occasions or interesting subjects. According to the practice of his Church, he was brought officially into intimate contact with all sorts and conditions of people, and his sympathy as well as his help was just as much at the service of the mill-hand, the servant girl, the jaded postman or policeman off their respective beats, as of those who brought trained intelligence, or influence, or charm of individuality with them.

It began to be understood that to relieve and to console were held by him not as a duty, but as a prerogative, and also that he was a man not easily tired or discouraged. To speak of him as self-denying would be a mistake, as that implies conflict and victory, and John was conscious of neither. Possibly the means he had at command,

for the wealthy draper was his son's almoner,
counted for something in the general sum of consideration, for money gives power not only in the
general sense, but through many delicate and
hidden springs of action and of feeling.

Simple and reticent as in his boyhood, and with
much of his boyhood's shyness and awkwardness
remaining, he had the gift of winning human trust
and confidence, so that sorrows that had rankled,
or shames that had burned inwardly for long years,
were yielded to his voice and took their balm of
healing at his hands.  He was the forlorn hope
in any official pressure or difficulty, being always
willing to do the one thing wanted, however
humble or obscure, without the interference of
personal predilections, for he recognised no grada-
tions in the Divine service.  It was said by some
who knew him best that John Cartwright was
never seen to such advantage in Castle Street
pulpit as when he served some little wayside
chapel and poured forth in gracious but uncon-

scious adaptation the rich stores of his mind and heart.

It was a curious fact, but an undoubted tribute to his personality, that Margery Denison, who had tasted the wine and gathered the roses of life, and had passed in review the elect of London society, conceived an interest, even an admiration, for the young Wesleyan minister which was introducing an element of disturbance into the monotony of her daily life.

Amongst Cyril Denison's forefathers had been men who had cut themselves adrift from the National Church when lying in the torpor of the eighteenth century, and who had lent their name and position to the support of the new movement which was then shaking the world from its slumber.

Therefore when he knew that his sister and his daughter were beginning to frequent Castle Street Chapel—taking out for the purpose that same carriage and pair of horses (very much the worse for long service) in which he and Margery had been seated when the two cousins first crossed their path—he raised no objections, contenting himself with a sneer at the poverty of their resources.

'You are quite right,' replied Margery; 'I go to chapel in default of any other function, and listen to John Cartwright because somehow or other he helps me to bear my life without breaking out into mutiny.'

'A life of your own choice, and of which I could desire the penalties were greater,' was his answer.

Margery smiled. 'And yet you do your best,' she said, and then immediately regretted the words as undutiful, and added impulsively: 'Forgive me! John Cartwright convinces me of sin. I should like to win you over and compel you to love me.'

'The means of performing the process that you describe as "winning me over" were in your own hands some time ago, and you rejected them. I scarcely think my life will be long enough, or fate so kind, as to give you another chance.'

Margery turned away with a feeling of hopeless defeat.

Her life just now was very weary. She had the feeling of being shut in bounds from which sooner or later she must escape. Under the influence of her best feelings she had refused the magnificent proposals of Lord Thimberley, and was now chafing under a feeling of self-contempt because she regretted passionately, not the action, indeed, but the consequences that it had entailed upon her in the added bitterness of her father's behaviour and the fretful complainings of her aunt.

It was under this pressure of weariness and isolation that she conceived the idea of asking Philippa Yorke on a visit to The Chace, always supposing that Mr. Denison would not put his veto on the proposal. There was a feverish desire in Margery's mind to bring about a union between

Gilbert Yorke and his cousin, the sources of which she did not examine too closely. Had she not fully disclosed them to her lover himself?

Mrs. Sutherland was fairly intimate with Mrs. Yorke, though Margery's knowledge of Philippa was of the slightest, and it was a letter to the former lady from the latter which had first suggested the idea of the invitation. Mrs. Yorke had mentioned that while Edward's health seemed to improve, as if in physical protest against the injustice of Sir Owen's will, Philippa was growing more and more ailing and delicate.

Undoubtedly the bracing air of Yorkshire, not to mention the proximity of Rookhurst, would do the invalid good.

Margery discussed the matter with her aunt, who, even more *ennuyée* than herself, was quite willing to enter into agreement, though doubting her brother's consent.

'There will be no difficulty with Mrs. Yorke,' she remarked. 'She will jump at the opportunity of sending the poor girl within easy reach of her cousin.'

It is the unexpected that always happens, as we know. To the surprise of both daughter and sister, Mr. Denison gave his consent to the proposal.

Possibly, in his own despite, he had been touched by Margery's kindness and forbearance, which were indeed noble at times; possibly he thought that the future mistress of Rookhurst—in which light all the world regarded Philippa—would be a not undesirable friend for his daughter in the dark days that were probably in store for her. Also he knew that his womankind would take good care that the stranger did not intrude on his privacy.

' You may do as you choose on the one condition that you keep her out of my way,' was his gracious concession.

So Margery despatched her invitation, couched in the most winning terms; and as she closed her letter and slipped it into the bag, she was conscious of a flutter of feeling hard to define.

'What, bare of all disguise, is my motive?' she asked herself anxiously. 'Is it magnanimity or discretion?'

# CHAPTER XIII.

IT was Saturday morning, an hour before the early dinner at Elm Lodge. Mrs. Cartwright was busy in her linen-closet, passing in review her stores of fine linen and finer damask, and laying out in her methodical manner the napery that would be required for the ensuing week.

It was one of her household duties that she relished most; indeed, it would not be too much to say that she derived more intimate pleasure from the sight of the glistening piles — each article daintily embroidered by her own fingers with the family monogram—than she would have done from the finest work of art. She had been known to remark to her female friends, with an air of chastened self-gratulation, that 'she never stained her linen with an ink-mark.' Perhaps if there was one satisfaction of this kind keener than another, it was the contemplation of her son's shirts.

Just at this period life was running with her on oiled wheels: her son was fulfilling the fondest ambitions and the most sacred aspirations she had cherished, the only drawback being a trembling fear lest he might fall within the scope of the ominous warning: 'Take heed when all men speak well of thee!'

There was still the rankling grievance of his extravagant regard for the worldling, Gilbert Yorke; but by common consent this was a subject rarely discussed between them, and John had passed the age when she could call him to account in respect to the spending of every hour of his time, although it must be conceded that this immunity was not unfrequently violated.

On Saturdays Martin Cartwright always dined

at his private house, and it was his son's habit so to arrange his own work as to be able to call for his father at his place of business, in order that they might walk home in company.

Therefore it was with a certain surprise this morning that Mrs. Cartwright heard the familiar click of the garden gate a full hour before the usual time, and, glancing hastily from the window which overlooked the garden, perceived her son walking up the gravel-path towards the house, and alone.

A sudden misgiving seized her; she went to the window that she might observé him more closely. As she did so, he looked up and smiled, with a little movement of the hand in greeting; but the action showed her that it was performed with difficulty and that he was very pale.

At that moment it seemed to Rachel Cartwright that she forestalled the unspeakable anguish which it had been her daily prayer as a mother to be spared, and a speechless cry rushed Godwards from her heart that He would avert the one blow to which her faith was not equal.

Then she struggled with herself for a few moments before she went downstairs to face the unknown trouble with due composure.

She found John sitting in the dining-room with his hat on the table beside him. To her watchful anxiety even this trifling circumstance seemed significant, for, as a matter of routine, it should have been hung up in the hall.

He looked towards her as she entered, but did not rise or smile; if he made an effort to speak, it was a fruitless one. She came close up to him and said in a voice of unnatural calm:

'What has happened? Try and tell me—are you taken suddenly ill?'

He did try, speaking with painful distinctness:

'No, but I have met with an accident. I have been knocked down by a steam-tram on the Seamoor Road. It is only the shock—no bones are broken—I have been able to walk home.'

She gazed at him with silent consternation. The pallor of the swarthy face, with its unmistakable look of pain, so moved her that she could scarcely control some untoward burst of feeling. Looking at him more narrowly, she saw that his coat was torn about the sleeve and shoulder.

'Are you sure no bones—are broken?' she asked. 'Did no one witness the accident, that you were allowed to walk home alone? But—I see! I will not ask you any questions.'

She turned swiftly to the sideboard, where a flagon of fresh water with glasses always stood, filled one of them, adding a little brandy from the well-stored cellaret below, and came back to his side.

'Drink this, dear,' she said quietly, 'and let me help you to the sofa. We must send for the doctor.'

'Do not move me,' he entreated; 'I am quite comfortable here, and better already.' He had drunk the mixture eagerly, and returned her the empty glass with a smile that seemed to confirm the assertion.

She assented, too wisely tender to press the point, and then, seeing that she might safely leave him alone, went out of the room to despatch a servant for medical help.

Left alone, John Cartwright, with his elbow heavily propped on the table beside him, covered his face with his hands. His lips moved, not in prayer, but in thanksgiving, that he had been the means of snatching from a horrible death, or from mutilation almost worse than death, the woman of his secret adoration.

How it had all happened he scarcely knew; the scene was one of confusion in his memory which he shrank from recalling.

He saw the hideous vehicle standing on the lines of the road along which his business lay, and at a point where there was a deep incline. The next moment he saw it in rapid motion and that, simultaneously, a tall girl, instantly recognised, attempted to cross the road in front of the advancing car.

Under ordinary conditions, at the distance which separated them she might have done this with safety; but from some strange negligence the driver had failed to apply the brake to his engine, and had consequently lost the power to regulate its downward impetus.

There are crises where the spirit animates the bodily powers almost to the point of miracle. Some paces separated John Cartwright from Margery Denison, but with a spring like that of some wild animal he reached her side in time to drag her back out of danger, receiving himself a blow from the buffer of the engine, which flung him happily beyond the line of rails. When the engineer was able to check his course, he saw that John had risen, and was evidently assuring his companion that he was unhurt; hence, he deemed it the wisest policy to pursue his way. The two were left standing alone in the comparative solitude of the road.

For a moment or two they looked speechlessly into each other's eyes; the conflict of feeling—of horror, of gratitude, and of anxiety—deprived Margery of any power of expression beyond the fixed, eager, passionate gaze. She was so deadly pale, and trembled so violently, that John was filled with a terror that deadened him to his own sensations.

'You are not hurt? It did not touch you?' he stammered.

'I! Do not speak of me!' she said, rallying her strength with a desperate effort. 'Are *you* hurt? That is the question. Lean against me for a moment, Mr. Cartwright. Oh, do not stand on idle scruples!'

As she spoke, being as tall as he, she passed her arm about his shoulders, and offered her slender but vigorous body as his prop, and he, dazed and bruised by the concussion, and with what consciousness was left rapt and bewildered, had no power but to accept her help.

For a few moments they stood thus. With her, every feeling was absorbed in gratitude and anxiety that reached the point of distress, while his sensations suggested to him the idea of a divine torture. Then, the difficulty of the situation stimulating him to exertion, he moved away from her a little and smiled.

'Thank you, I am better, much better! I think I can walk home. You are quite sure you are not hurt?'

She disregarded the question, her attention being riveted on his movements.

'You are not deceiving me? You are really better? I pray God you may only have suffered a shock; but that is too much! Can you move your arms, Mr. Cartwright? Can you walk? Just a little—to ease my mind!'

'Perfectly. You see that I can!' returning to the spot where she was standing, and stretching out first one arm and then the other to reassure her. He found the process sufficiently painful, but the result convinced him that he really had escaped without broken bones.

Then Margery took out her handkerchief and, in spite of his protest, began to wipe off assiduously the dust that had gathered on his clothes.

'What will you do?' she asked. 'There is no cab to be seen, of course, and I am sure you will not be able to walk home.'

'I am quite able; our house is little more than a quarter of an hour's walk from here, and I would not take a cab on any account—it would alarm my mother. What I most regret is that I cannot see you to a place of safety.'

'You will be able to do that. I am going in your direction, and we will walk together. I beseech you, Mr. Cartwright, to lean on my arm; I am not one of the weak women.'

Her voice shook; for a moment her lips quivered. From what a horrible death he had saved her, and at what risk to himself! She conquered the weakness, knowing that if she yielded at all she would break down ignominiously.

A few people passed them on the road, but there was not much in their appearance to challenge curiosity. John had soon withdrawn himself from Margery's arm, and the damage to his dress was not conspicuous.

By virtue of a painful effort he was able to walk by her side without faltering, the intense anxiety her looks and words conveyed giving him the necessary courage, and filling his mind with a gratitude that touched on worship. His own action seemed of so little account, and the recognition so disproportionate.

About half-way to Elm Lodge the road diverged into three cross-ways, one of them leading to the Vicarage, where it had been Margery's intention to call. She wished to give up her visit and accompany John to his own house, but he opposed the idea strenuously.

'You cannot walk home without rest and re-

freshment, Miss Denison,' he said, ' and here it is
close at hand.   It will be the greatest relief to me
to think of you as under shelter.   You will promise
not to return by the same route alone.'

He shuddered involuntarily, and grew very pale.

' I promise.   I am going to spend the day with
Mrs. Stansfield, and my people send the carriage
for me this evening.   I think it will be best to
carry out the arrangement.   But I am quite equal
to going home with you and coming back again.
You do not like the idea ?   You mean that you
wish us to part here ?   That you *prefer* to go
home alone ?'

He signified assent, then added :

' My mother would be alarmed if she saw us
together.'

' And why should she not be alarmed ?' demanded Margery.   ' She will need to thank God
to-day as she has never thanked God before, first
for giving her such a son, and then for sparing him
to her.   As for me, I am your bondslave for life !'

Tears filled her eyes as she held out both her hands to him.

As he took them and let them fall with a slight respectful pressure he remembered that it was almost precisely on this spot that she had given the same greeting to Gilbert Yorke on the first occasion that he himself had seen her. The thought checked the ardour of the words that had sprung to his lips.

'Ah,' she said, with a slightly disappointed air, 'you are used to saving souls, and think less of redeeming one poor girl from bodily destruction than she could wish. However, I shall try and make Mrs. Cartwright understand. Please tell her that nothing will satisfy me but to be allowed to make my inquiries in person to-morrow.'

And so they had parted, Margery continuing to stand at the cross-ways to watch John's progress so long as he was in sight, and he, fully aware of the fact, keeping up appearances, until a turn of the road relieved him of a strain that had become well-nigh intolerable.

It took him more than half an hour to reach his mother's door, and by that time his fortitude and strength were equally exhausted.

The next day it was known far and wide that an accident had happened to the Rev. John Cartwright, but it was not known that the injuries had been sustained in behalf of another.

John did not mention Miss Denison, and she had not redeemed her promise of a call. It was true a message of inquiry had been received from The Chace, but it was in Mrs. Sutherland's name, and was accepted by Mrs. Cartwright as an index of the respect in which her son was held.

The doctors had definitely pronounced that their patient had broken no bones, but contused bruises and shock to the system were perhaps ills of quite as serious a nature, and would demand care and skilful nursing.

John submitted to his bed and to seclusion with

a readiness that increased his mother's apprehensions; but after a day or two she was persuaded to dismiss her fears, and then, it must be owned, she rather enjoyed the situation. She would allow no one to wait upon him but herself, and she welcomed the opportunity given to her for exclusively enjoying her son's society, until her vigilance detected that he appeared to be under a cloud.

At first she supposed it was some spiritual trouble, and she questioned him as closely as her growing reverence and his constitutional reserve would permit, but he reassured her on this point.

' Then you suffer more pain than you confess or than the doctors allow ?'

' Oh no ! I have some pain, of course, but it is nothing, and is less every day. I shall soon have forgotten all about it. Do not worry about me, mother.'

He smiled and pressed her hand, but she little

knew what agonies of suppressed irritability her ceaseless watchfulness caused him.

He was fighting a desperate battle with himself.

The deep impression which Margery had made upon him as a boy had been stamped even more sharply as time went on, owing to the sustained though secret oversight of her life claimed from his friendship by Gilbert Yorke. The two recent occasions on which he had seen and talked with her, and the last fateful incident, had all given added strength to his feeling for her, until it had grown outside his control, and gathered the force of a passion.

Neither conscience the most exacting nor the strictest demands of religion can forbid the rising of a young man's love to the spring-tide of yearning and pain. He knew that she was not for him, but that did not lessen by a hair's breadth the strength of the mad craving to possess her. Could some impossible conjunction of circumstances have given him what was the desire of his eyes as well as of his heart, his loyalty to his friend would have enabled him to turn his back on his opportunity; but that made the stings of passion and of pain no whit easier to bear.

As he lay motionless in bed, sometimes feigning sleep as a safeguard against interruption, he lived over and over again every point and detail of what had happened. He saw her as he had seen her the moment before the accident, walking as no other girl walked, removed to an atmosphere of her own by her sweet composure and stately loveliness—aloof from every-day humanity; the next, composure and stateliness had vanished—the sudden pallor, the wide-eyed anguish, the poignant note of her delicious voice, were not the outcome of personal terror, but of a sympathy so warm and eager that, as he recalled it, his heart beat with a sense of suffocation.

How fine and wide the nature must be that could thus identify itself with the danger of another, almost a stranger, and, by all social laws, her inferior! How generous the heart in which gratitude rose to the height of a passion !

It was with a sort of divine shame that he recalled the touch of her sustaining arm, the sweet womanliness with which she had placed her superb strength at his service, and the be-wildering extravagance of phrase in which her recognition of what he had done for her had found voice :

' As for me, I am your bondslave for life !'

He repeated the words softly to himself with a smile sadder than tears. It was a splendid hyper-bole for a fine lady to use towards the man who had saved her life, but for the man himself it was a bare statement of truth.

' I think I have always loved her—I know that I always shall.'

That she had spoken and acted under the strong excitement of the moment was evident (if evidence were needed), since she had not called on his mother according to her promise. He was glad of it. It spared him inevitable cross-examination — quite natural, but none the less trying—and left him the earnest hope that her share in the accident might always remain unknown.

END OF VOL. II.

BILLING AND SONS, PRINTERS, GUILDFORD